bring these two hearts together. As romance blossoms between stolen moments of holiday baking and winter walks, Stephanie discovers she's not just inheriting a bakery—she's stepping into a rich history that will change her life forever.

When renowned chef Helena Drake arrives in town, bringing her sharp city attitude and hidden connections to Sweet Pine Valley's past, the story deepens. Together, they uncover a treasure trove of old recipes, family secrets, and a legacy of love that spans generations.

As Christmas approaches in this enchanting Vermont town, Stephanie must decide if she's ready to embrace not just a new business and a new love, but a destiny she never knew was waiting for her. With the help of a nervous dachshund, a determined veteran chef, and the discovery of long-lost family connections, she learns that sometimes the sweetest dreams are the ones you never knew you had.

"A Sweet Season of Love" is a heartwarming tale that proves home isn't just a place—it's where love takes root and blooms. Perfect for fans of Debbie Macomber and Susan Mallery, this charming story combines the warmth of small-town life with the magic of holiday romance and the sweet satisfaction of finding exactly where you belong.

Fall in love with Sweet Pine Valley, where every recipe tells a story and every heart finds its way home.

Sweet Pine Valley Holiday Recipe Collection

AF093703

Fields of Sweet Dreams Holiday Recipe Collection

Elizabeth's Perfect Pumpkin Pie

As discovered in Elizabeth Fields' recipe journal

Ingredients for Crust:

- 2½ cups all-purpose flour
- 1 teaspoon salt
- 1 tablespoon sugar
- 1 cup cold unsalted butter, cubed
- ¼ to ½ cup ice water
- 1 egg wash (1 egg beaten with 1 tablespoon water)

Ingredients for Filling:

- 2 cups pumpkin puree (freshly roasted or canned)
- 3 large eggs
- 1¼ cups heavy cream
- ¾ cup packed brown sugar
- 2 tablespoons maple syrup
- 1 tablespoon vanilla extract
- 1½ teaspoons ground cinnamon
- ½ teaspoon ground ginger
- ¼ teaspoon ground nutmeg
- ¼ teaspoon ground cloves
- ½ teaspoon salt

Instructions:

1. For the crust:

Where dreams rise like fresh-baked bread and love blooms in unexpected places...

When New York-trained pastry chef Stephanie Fields fled to the small town of Sweet Pine Valley, she was looking for a fresh start, not a legacy. But her newly purchased bakery, Fields of Sweet Dreams, holds more than just sugar and spice—it carries the stories of two remarkable women who came before her.

Handsome local veterinarian Jack Carter isn't looking for love either, but fate has other plans when his sister's timid rescue dachshund, Tessa, helps bring these two hearts together. As romance blossoms between stolen moments of holiday baking and winter walks, Stephanie discovers she's not just inheriting a bakery—she's stepping into a rich history that will change her life forever.

When renowned chef Helena Drake arrives in town, bringing her sharp city attitude and hidden connections to Sweet Pine Valley's past, the story deepens. Together, they uncover a treasure trove of old recipes, family secrets, and a legacy of love that spans generations.

As Christmas approaches in this enchanting Vermont town, Stephanie must decide if she's ready to embrace not just a new business and a new love, but a destiny she never knew was waiting for her. With the help of a nervous dachshund, a determined veteran chef, and the discovery of long-lost family connections, she learns that sometimes the sweetest dreams are the ones you never knew you had.

"A Sweet Season of Love" is a heartwarming tale that proves home isn't just a place—it's where love takes root and blooms. Perfect for fans of Debbie Macomber and Susan Mallery, this charming story combines the warmth of small-town life with the magic of holiday romance and the sweet satisfaction of finding exactly where you belong.

Patti Petrone Miller

Fall in love with Sweet Pine Valley, where every recipe tells a story and every heart finds its way home.

EDITORIAL REVIEW
"Patti Petrone Miller's books hit different than your typical feel-good stories. Sure, Hallmark's got their formula down pat, but Miller brings something fresh to the table - authentic characters that actually feel like people you know, dealing with real-life stuff while still keeping things wonderfully uplifting.
I honestly get the same warm fuzzies reading her books as I do curling up with hot cocoa for a Hallmark marathon, but without all the predictable plot points we've seen a million times. She's nailed that sweet spot between heartwarming and genuine that's super hard to find these days. If you're looking for stories that'll leave you smiling but don't make you roll your eyes at how perfect everything is, Miller's your girl. She's got that special touch that makes you feel like you're hanging out with friends rather than just reading about characters. Move over, Hallmark - "there's a new queen of wholesome in town!"

Where dreams rise like fresh-baked bread and love blooms in unexpected places...

When New York-trained pastry chef Stephanie Fields fled to the small town of Sweet Pine Valley, she was looking for a fresh start, not a legacy. But her newly purchased bakery, Fields of Sweet Dreams, holds more than just sugar and spice—it carries the stories of two remarkable women who came before her.

Handsome local veterinarian Jack Carter isn't looking for love either, but fate has other plans when his sister's timid rescue dachshund, Tessa, helps

- Combine flour, salt, and sugar in a food processor
- Pulse in cold butter until mixture resembles coarse meal
- Add ice water gradually until dough forms
- Chill for at least 1 hour

2. For the filling:
   - Whisk pumpkin puree and eggs until smooth
   - Add cream, brown sugar, maple syrup, and vanilla
   - Mix in spices and salt until well combined
3. Assembly:
   - Roll out dough and fit into 9-inch pie dish
   - Crimp edges decoratively
   - Brush edges with egg wash
   - Pour in filling
   - Bake at 425°F for 15 minutes
   - Reduce temperature to 350°F and bake 40-45 minutes more
   - Cool completely before serving

Sweet Pine Valley Heritage Turkey

Adapted from Sophie Drake's family recipes

Ingredients:

- 1 (12-14 lb) fresh turkey
- 1 cup butter, softened
- 2 tablespoons fresh sage, chopped
- 2 tablespoons fresh thyme leaves
- 2 tablespoons fresh rosemary, chopped
- 3 tablespoons garlic, minced
- 2 tablespoons kosher salt
- 1 tablespoon black pepper

- 2 apples, quartered
- 2 onions, quartered
- 1 lemon, quartered
- Fresh herbs for cavity

Herb Butter Instructions:

1. Mix softened butter with herbs, garlic, salt, and pepper
2. Gently separate skin from turkey breast
3. Rub herb butter mixture under skin and all over turkey

Roasting Instructions:

1. Preheat oven to 425°F
2. Stuff cavity with apples, onions, lemon, and fresh herbs
3. Tie legs together and tuck wings
4. Roast for 30 minutes at 425°F
5. Reduce temperature to 350°F
6. Baste every 30 minutes
7. Cook until internal temperature reaches 165°F (about 15 minutes per pound)
8. Rest for 20-30 minutes before carving

Helena's Modern Traditional Stuffing

Ingredients:

- 1 large loaf crusty bread, cubed and dried overnight
- 4 tablespoons butter
- 2 onions, diced
- 4 celery stalks, diced
- 2 apples, diced
- 4 garlic cloves, minced

- 2 tablespoons fresh sage, chopped
- 2 tablespoons fresh thyme leaves
- 1 tablespoon fresh rosemary, chopped
- 1 cup dried cranberries
- 1 cup pecans, toasted and chopped
- 3-4 cups chicken or vegetable broth
- 2 eggs, beaten
- Salt and pepper to taste

Instructions:

1. Sauté vegetables and apples in butter until tender
2. Add garlic and herbs, cook until fragrant
3. Combine with bread cubes, cranberries, and pecans
4. Mix in broth gradually until bread is moist but not soggy
5. Stir in beaten eggs
6. Transfer to greased baking dish
7. Bake at 350°F covered for 30 minutes
8. Uncover and bake 15-20 minutes more until top is golden

Fields of Sweet Dreams Gingerbread House

A collaboration between Elizabeth Fields and Helena Drake's techniques

Ingredients for Gingerbread:

- 6 cups all-purpose flour
- 1 tablespoon ground ginger
- 1 tablespoon ground cinnamon
- 1 teaspoon ground nutmeg
- 1 teaspoon ground cloves
- ½ teaspoon salt
- 1½ cups unsalted butter

- 1½ cups packed dark brown sugar
- 2 large eggs
- 1 cup dark molasses
- 1 tablespoon vanilla extract

Royal Icing:

- 4 cups powdered sugar
- 3 egg whites
- ½ teaspoon cream of tartar
- 1 teaspoon vanilla extract

Instructions:

1. Gingerbread Dough:
     - Whisk dry ingredients
     - Cream butter and sugar
     - Add eggs, molasses, and vanilla
     - Gradually mix in dry ingredients
     - Chill dough 2 hours minimum
2. House Templates:
     - Front/back: 6x8 inches with peaked top
     - Sides: 6x8 inches rectangle
     - Roof: 7x9 inches rectangle
     - Optional: door, windows, chimney
3. Construction:
     - Roll dough ¼ inch thick
     - Cut pieces using templates
     - Bake at 350°F for 12-15 minutes
     - Cool completely
     - Assemble with royal icing
     - Let dry 24 hours before decorating
4. Decoration Suggestions:

Barking Up The Wrong Bakery, Thanksgiving

- Candy canes for posts
- Shredded coconut for snow
- Small candies for lights
- Pretzel sticks for logs
- Cereal squares for roof tiles

Notes for Success:
- Keep royal icing covered when not in use
- Use heavy paper or cardboard for templates
- Work in stages over 2-3 days
- Store finished house in cool, dry place

Remember, as Helena always says, "Precision in preparation leads to perfection in presentation."

Authors Book List

Accidental Vows
A Krampus Christmas
Sin Takes A Holiday
Barking Up The Wrong Bakery, Thankgiving
Barking Up The Wrong Bakery, Christmas
Best Served Dead
Bewitching Charms
Christmas at Hollybrook Inn
Christmas on Peppermit Lane
Krampus
Hex and the City
Love in Stitches
Pies and Perps

Patti Petrone Miller

Spectres and Souffles
Mamma Mia It's Murder
Once Upon A Christmas
The Fatman
The Frosted Felony
The Purr-fect Suspect
The Boogeyman
The Gingerdead Men
Vikings Enchantress
Welcome to Scarecrow Hollow
The Pendleton Witches
The Cabinet of Curiosities
Christmas In Pine Haven
Love in the Stacks
Once Upon A Christmas

Barking Up The Wrong Bakery

Thanksgiving

Book One

by Patti Petrone Miller

AP Miller Productions

Patti Petrone Miller

(Barking Up The Wrong Bakery, Thanksgiving)
First Edition Copyright © November 2024 by Patti Petrone Miller

No part of this publication may be reproduced, stored in a retrieval system, or transmitted, in any form or by any means, without the prior permission in writing of the publisher, nor be otherwise circulated in any form of binding or cover other than that in which it is published and without a similar condition including this condition being imposed on the subsequent purchaser.

FBI Anti-Piracy Warning: The unauthorized reproduction or distribution of a copyrighted work is illegal.

Criminal copyright infringement, including infringement without monetary gain, is investigated by the FBI and is punishable by up to five years in federal prison and a fine of $250,000.

Cover art by TMT Book Cover Designs

Published by AP Miller Productions All rights reserved.

Your support of the author's rights is appreciated.

For my beautiful puppy, Tessa for whom this book was written

12/28/2006- 11/20/2023

Patti Petrone Miller

Chapter 1

New Begnnings

The twinkling lights of Sweet Pine Valley's Main Street reflected off the freshly fallen snow, creating a magical glow that made Stephanie Fields pause in her work. Her fingers, dusted with flour and sugar, traced the delicate engagement ring on her left hand – a vintage piece with a snowflake design that Jack had discovered in his grandmother's jewelry box. The memory of his Christmas Eve proposal last year, surrounded by gingerbread houses and twinkling lights, still made her heart flutter.

Through the bakery's front window of Fields of Sweet Dreams, she could see the town coming alive with Thanksgiving decorations. Mr. Henderson from the hardware store was hanging wreaths made by the local garden club, while Mrs. Thompson from the book shop arranged fall-themed displays. This little town had become more than just a place she'd escaped to after leaving her high-powered marketing career in the city – it had become home.

The familiar jingle of bells at the door made her heart skip, followed by the clickety-clack of tiny paws on hardwood floors. Tessa, their newly adopted dachshund, trotted in wearing a festive orange and brown sweater that Stephanie's mother had knitted, her long body wiggling with excitement despite her usual timidity. Behind her, Jack Carter – her fiancé and the town's beloved veterinarian – carried two steaming cups of peppermint hot chocolate from Clara's Coffee Corner across the street.

"There's my favorite girls," Jack said, his blue eyes crinkling at the corners in that way that still made Stephanie's knees weak. His dark hair was dusted with snowflakes, and his cheeks were flushed from the cold. He set the cups down on the vintage counter that they'd refinished together over the summer, a project that had ended in more paint fights than actual painting.

Tessa, still adjusting after her recent adoption from Jack's sister Sarah, stayed close to his legs but wagged her tail at Stephanie. The little dachshund had come into their lives unexpectedly, much like love itself had for both of them.

"Someone's getting braver," Stephanie noted, kneeling down with a small piece of dog-safe sugar cookie shaped like a maple leaf. Tessa cautiously approached, her nose twitching at the treat. "Remember how she wouldn't even come out from behind the counter that first day?"

"Just like someone else I know," Jack smiled, his voice soft with memory. He reached out and tucked a loose strand of Stephanie's honey-blonde hair behind her ear, his touch lingering on her cheek. "Who would've thought a broken oven, a winter storm, and one nervous little dachshund would change our lives forever?"

Stephanie leaned into his touch, remembering that fateful day last year when Jack had come to fix her ancient oven just before the holiday rush. He'd ended up stranded at the bakery during a surprise blizzard, and they'd spent the night baking by candlelight and sharing stories of their lives. "You were quite the hero that night, Dr. Carter," she teased. "Fixing both my oven and my belief in Christmas miracles."

"Well, Ms. Soon-to-be-Carter," he pulled her close, the scent of his wool sweater mixing with the bakery's warm spices, "you were the one who showed me that home isn't just a place – it's a feeling."

Stephanie stood, brushing flour from her vintage-inspired apron – the one Jack had given her for her birthday, with "Fields of Sweet Dreams" embroidered in rustic script. "Speaking of feelings, are you ready for tomorrow? First Thanksgiving as an officially engaged couple, hosting both our families..."

"And don't forget the annual Sweet Pine Valley Thanksgiving Festival baking competition," Jack reminded her, his hands resting on her waist. "Though I still think entering Tessa in the pet costume parade was a bold move."

"She'll be the cutest hot dog in a pilgrim costume this town has ever seen," Stephanie laughed, watching as Tessa finally gathered the courage to explore the bakery's kitchen, her nose leading her to a basket of fallen pie crust pieces. "Besides, Sarah said it might help build her confidence."

Jack pulled Stephanie closer, swaying slightly as if dancing to the soft holiday music playing from the bakery's vintage radio. "You know what I love most about you?" he murmured against her hair. "How you can take something broken – whether it's an old bakery, a timid dachshund, or a small-town vet who'd given up on finding love – and make it whole again."

"Jack Carter, are you getting sentimental on me?" Stephanie teased, though her eyes misted over. She reached up to straighten his collar, a habit she'd developed during their countless morning goodbyes.

"Must be all these holiday spices going to my head," he chuckled, but his eyes were serious as they met hers. "Or maybe it's just knowing that this year, I finally have everything I never knew I needed."

As evening approached, snowflakes began to dance outside the bakery windows, creating nature's own snow globe around their cozy haven. Stephanie gazed at her engagement ring, thinking about how different this holiday season would be from the last. No more lonely nights in her apartment above the bakery – now she had a family: Jack, Tessa, and the whole Carter clan who had welcomed her with open arms and secret family recipes.

Tessa, having found her confidence, hopped onto the window seat to watch the snow, her small body silhouetted against the twilight sky. Her adoption papers – framed in the apartment upstairs – marked the official beginning of their little family, though their hearts had been knit together long before the ink dried.

Jack wrapped his arms around Stephanie from behind, and they both watched their little family's newest member. The bakery's warmth enveloped them, along with the lingering scent of the snickerdoodles they'd made together that morning – Jack's grandmother's recipe, now part of their shared legacy.

"You know," Jack whispered, his breath warm against her ear, "sometimes the best gifts come in unexpected packages."

"Like a timid dachshund and a small-town vet?" Stephanie smiled, leaning back into his embrace, feeling the steady beat of his heart against her back.

"And a baker who makes the best snickerdoodles in three counties," Jack added, kissing her cheek. "Who knew that broken oven would lead to a perfectly baked happily-ever-after?"

As the first stars appeared in the November sky, Tessa let out a contented sigh, finally at home with her forever family. Tomorrow would bring the chaos of holiday preparations, family celebrations, and the festival, but for now, in the warmth of the bakery, everything was perfect – just like a sweet dusting of sugar on one of Stephanie's famous cookies.

The town clock chimed six, its melody mixing with the holiday music and the soft whir of the bakery's mixers. Outside, Sweet Pine Valley transformed into a Christmas card scene, while inside Fields of Sweet Dreams, three hearts beat as one, proving that sometimes the sweetest recipes are the ones life writes itself.

Chapter 2

Turkey Troubles and Sugar-Coated Surprises

Thanksgiving morning dawned with the kind of perfect snowfall that seemed to exist only in snow globes and holiday movies. Stephanie woke to the sound of Tessa's paws padding across the hardwood floors of the apartment above Fields of Sweet Dreams, followed by Jack's muffled voice cooing at their four-legged alarm clock.

"Come on, princess, let Mom sleep a little longer," Jack whispered, but Tessa had other ideas. The little dachshund managed to nose open the bedroom door, launching herself onto the bed with surprising agility for her tiny legs. She burrowed under the quilts – a wedding gift from Jack's grandmother that they'd decided to use early – until she found Stephanie's face and proceeded to shower her with good morning kisses.

"I tried," Jack laughed from the doorway, holding two steaming mugs of coffee. He was already dressed in what Stephanie called his "festival finest" – a crisp blue button-down that matched his eyes, paired with dark jeans and his lucky boots. "But someone insisted on starting Thanksgiving preparations exactly at six AM."

Stephanie sat up, accepting both the coffee and a good morning kiss from Jack. "Well, she's not wrong. We have a lot to do before everyone arrives." She took a sip of coffee, perfectly prepared with a dash of cinnamon and maple syrup – just one of the countless little ways Jack showed his love. "Did you remember to take the turkey out of the freezer last night?"

The way Jack's eyes widened told her everything she needed to know.

"Jack Carter!" Stephanie swung her legs out of bed, nearly spilling her coffee. "That turkey needed to defrost for days!"

"Now, honey, before you panic—" Jack began, but Stephanie was already racing down the back stairs to their kitchen, Tessa hot on her heels, her little legs working overtime to keep up.

The kitchen, usually Stephanie's sanctuary of sweet-smelling order, was about to become ground zero for their first major couple crisis since the Great Christmas Tree Debate of last December (artificial versus real – they'd compromised with a real tree for the bakery and artificial for their apartment). She yanked open the freezer door to find a thoroughly frozen twenty-pound turkey staring back at her.

"Okay," Jack appeared behind her, wrapping his arms around her waist. "So I may have forgotten about the turkey. But remember what you always say about every kitchen disaster being an opportunity for creativity?"

Stephanie turned in his arms, trying to maintain her panic but failing as she caught the twinkle in his eye. "Are you actually using my own baking philosophy against me, Dr. Carter?"

"Is it working?" He grinned, dropping a kiss on her nose.

Before she could answer, the bakery's front bell chimed. They both froze – the bakery wasn't supposed to open today.

"Hello?" Sarah's voice called out. "Anyone home? I brought reinforcements!"

Jack's sister appeared in the kitchen doorway, arms laden with grocery bags, her husband Tom behind her with what appeared to be—

"Is that a fully defrosted turkey?" Stephanie gasped.

Sarah grinned, setting down her bags. "Jack texted me last night in a panic. Apparently, someone's been a little distracted lately with festival preparations and wedding planning." She winked at her brother. "Lucky for you, Tom always buys an extra turkey. Something about being prepared for poultry emergencies."

"You knew about this?" Stephanie turned to Jack, who had the grace to look sheepish.

"I may have had a backup plan," he admitted. "Though I was kind of hoping I'd remember to defrost ours and we could donate the extra one to the community center's Thanksgiving dinner."

Stephanie felt her heart melt a little more – something she hadn't thought possible. Even in his forgetfulness, Jack was thinking of others. "We can still do that," she said. "Once ours defrosts, we'll take it over. Mrs. Henderson said they're expecting a record turnout this year."

"That's our cue to start cooking," Sarah announced, beginning to unpack her bags. "Tom, why don't you and Jack take Tessa for her morning walk and then head to the festival grounds? They could probably use some help setting up the judge's table for the baking competition."

As if understanding she was about to go for a walk, Tessa emerged from under the industrial mixer where she'd been hiding from all the commotion. Her tail wagged hopefully as she looked between Jack and Tom.

"What do you say, girl?" Jack knelt down, scratching behind her ears. "Want to help Uncle Tom test out the festival grounds?" At the word 'festival,' Tessa's entire body wiggled with excitement.

"Don't forget her pilgrim costume!" Stephanie called as the men headed upstairs to get Tessa's leash. "The pet parade is at two!"

Once they were alone, Sarah turned to Stephanie with a knowing smile. "So, how are you really doing? And don't give me that 'everything's perfect' line. I lived above this bakery for two years before Tom and I bought our house – I know how overwhelming holiday rushes can be."

Stephanie sighed, sinking onto a nearby stool. "Is it that obvious?"

"Only to someone who's been there," Sarah assured her, pulling out a second stool. "Talk to me."

"It's just..." Stephanie gestured around the kitchen, "all of this. The festival, Thanksgiving, the wedding planning, trying to make sure Tessa feels secure in her new home... I want everything to be perfect. Your family has such beautiful holiday traditions, and I—"

"Want to live up to them?" Sarah finished. When Stephanie nodded, Sarah reached over and squeezed her hand. "You know what one of my favorite Carter family traditions is? Making mistakes. Big, messy, hilarious mistakes that we laugh about for years. Like the time Mom tried to deep-fry a turkey and nearly set the garage on fire. Or when Jack attempted to make gingerbread men for his fourth-grade class and created what Dad still calls 'The Cookie Monster Massacre of '99.'"

Stephanie couldn't help but laugh. "He never told me about that!"

"Oh, honey, just wait until Mom breaks out the photo albums later. But my point is, you don't have to be perfect. You just have to be you – the amazing woman who made my brother happier than I've ever seen him, who turned this bakery into the heart of Sweet Pine Valley, and who's giving my formerly anxious rescue dog the best life imaginable."

As if summoned by the conversation, they heard Tessa's excited barking from upstairs, followed by Jack's laugh and what sounded suspiciously like something falling over.

"Speaking of your formerly anxious rescue dog," Stephanie grinned, "she's certainly found her voice."

"She's not the only one," Sarah said softly. "You know, when Jack first told me he was thinking of proposing, I asked him what made him so sure. You know what he said? He said that you taught him that home isn't just a place where you keep your things – it's where you keep your heart. And his heart has belonged to you since that first night in the bakery."

Stephanie felt tears welling up, but before she could respond, they heard the guys clomping back down the stairs, Tessa leading the way in her little plaid sweater.

"Ladies," Tom announced with exaggerated formality, "we're off to ensure the structural integrity of the judging table. No one wants a repeat of last year's Great Pie Collapse."

"That was one time!" Jack protested. "And I fixed it!"

"With duct tape and a prayer," Sarah muttered, making Stephanie giggle.

Jack crossed to Stephanie, pulling her in for a quick kiss. "You okay? You look like you might have been crying."

"Happy tears," she assured him, straightening his collar. "Your sister was just reminding me why I love being part of this family."

"Speaking of family," he said, "Mom called. They'll be here around noon with enough side dishes to feed half the town."

"Perfect timing for the festival," Stephanie nodded. "Did you remind her about—"

"Her famous cranberry sauce? Only about ten times. And Dad's bringing his special spiced cider for the bakery's hot drink station."

"And my parents?"

"Flight landed on time in Burlington. Uncle Pete is picking them up, and they'll be here by eleven." Jack kissed her again. "Stop worrying. Everything's going to be perfect."

"Or perfectly imperfect," Sarah chimed in with a wink.

"That too," Jack agreed. "Come on, Tom. Let's go make sure that judging table can withstand Mom's sweet potato casserole. Tessa, coming?"

The little dachshund looked between Jack and Stephanie, clearly torn.

"Go on, sweetheart," Stephanie encouraged. "Help Daddy make sure everything's safe for the festival."

That seemed to decide it. Tessa trotted to Jack's side, head held high as if she'd been tasked with an important mission.

Once the guys and Tessa had left, Sarah and Stephanie turned their attention to the morning's tasks. As they worked side by side – preparing stuffing, peeling potatoes, and starting the pies for both their family dinner and the festival competition – Stephanie felt a deep sense of contentment settle over her.

The kitchen filled with warmth and laughter as Sarah shared more Carter family stories. They lost track of time until the bell chimed again, this time announcing the arrival of Jack's parents, Richard and Marie Carter, laden with dishes and hugs.

"There's our girl!" Marie exclaimed, somehow managing to hug Stephanie despite her full arms. "Sarah, honey, help your father with the cider before he drops it. He insisted on carrying everything at once."

"It's called efficiency," Richard protested good-naturedly, allowing Sarah to relieve him of several containers.

"It's called stubbornness," Marie countered, "and speaking of stubborn Carters, where's my son and my granddogs?"

"Dog, Mom," Sarah corrected. "Singular. Unless there's something Jack and Stephanie haven't told us?"

Marie's eyes lit up hopefully, but Stephanie quickly jumped in. "Just Tessa for now. And she's helping Jack and Tom set up at the festival grounds."

"Well, we'll see her at the pet parade," Marie said, already rolling up her sleeves to help with the cooking. "Now, what can I do? And don't say nothing, Stephanie Fields. You're family now, which means you have to let us help."

The next hour passed in a blur of preparation, with more family arriving in waves. Stephanie's parents, David and Lauren Fields, arrived right on schedule, bringing with them the familiar scent of her mother's signature vanilla extract and her father's booming laugh.

The apartment above the bakery quickly filled with the kind of organized chaos that only families can create. Every surface in both the bakery kitchen and the apartment kitchen was covered with dishes in various stages of preparation. The smell of roasting turkey (the backup one, thankfully) mingled with pumpkin pie spices and cranberry sauce.

At one point, Stephanie escaped downstairs to check on the pies for the festival competition. In the quiet of her bakery, she took a moment to breathe, taking in the sight of the display cases filled with Thanksgiving-themed treats and the window decorations she and Jack had put up last weekend.

"Penny for your thoughts?"

She turned to find Jack in the doorway, cheeks ruddy from the cold, Tessa at his feet.

"Just thinking about how different everything is from last Thanksgiving," she said, welcoming them both into her arms. "Last year I was alone in this kitchen, stress-baking enough pies to feed an army because I didn't know what else to do with myself."

"And this year?" Jack prompted, though his smile suggested he knew the answer.

"This year I'm still baking enough pies to feed an army, but now it's because I have an army to feed." She leaned into him, feeling Tessa press against their legs. "A rather wonderful, slightly crazy army of people I love."

"Speaking of crazy," Jack pulled back slightly, reaching into his pocket. "I have something for you. An early Thanksgiving gift."

"Jack, we said no gifts—"

"It's not exactly a gift," he interrupted, pulling out a small, wrapped package. "More of a good luck charm for the baking competition."

Stephanie unwrapped it carefully to find a delicate silver charm in the shape of a rolling pin. "It's beautiful," she breathed.

"Turn it over."

Engraved on the back were the words: "Life is what you bake of it."

"Because you taught me that the best recipes," Jack said softly, "are the ones life writes itself."

Upstairs, they could hear their families laughing, the sounds of holiday preparation in full swing. Outside, Sweet

Pine Valley was coming alive with festival excitement. And there in the bakery where their story began, Stephanie Fields kissed Jack Carter while their little dachshund wagged her tail in approval.

Some might say it was just another Thanksgiving in a small town. But for Stephanie, Jack, and Tessa, it was something much more precious: it was the beginning of their own tradition, their own recipe for happiness, with just the right mixture of love, family, and a dash of sugar-coated chaos to make it perfectly imperfect.

Chapter 3

Sweet Victories & Tender Moments

The Sweet Pine Valley Town Square had transformed into a Thanksgiving wonderland. Strings of twinkling lights crisscrossed overhead, their glow reflecting off the fresh snow. Wooden stalls decorated with autumn garlands and mini pumpkins lined the square, offering everything from hot apple cider to handcrafted wreaths. At the center stood the judges' table for the baking competition – thoroughly reinforced, thanks to Jack and Tom's morning efforts.

"Ready for the big moment?" Jack squeezed Stephanie's hand as they approached the festival grounds. She carried her competition entry – a triple-layer pumpkin spice cake with maple cream cheese frosting and candied pecans – in a specially designed carrier. Tessa trotted beside them, already dressed in her pilgrim costume, complete with a tiny black hat and white collar.

"I think so," Stephanie nodded, though her voice wavered slightly. "Though I'm more nervous about Tessa's parade debut than the baking competition."

As if understanding she was the topic of conversation, Tessa gave a little bounce, her costume's buckle jingling. The transformation in their little dachshund over the past weeks had been remarkable. The formerly timid rescue now greeted each new adventure with cautious enthusiasm, much like Stephanie herself had learned to do.

"Speaking of debuts," Stephanie's mother appeared beside them, camera in hand, "the local newspaper wants to do a feature on Fields of Sweet Dreams for their holiday edition. Something about 'Sweet Pine Valley's Rising Star Baker and Her Picture-Perfect Life.'"

"Mom—" Stephanie began, but she was interrupted by the arrival of Jack's parents.

"Picture-perfect?" Marie Carter laughed warmly, adjusting her festive scarf. "Oh honey, wait until they hear about the turkey incident."

"Which will remain a family secret," Jack interjected quickly, throwing a pleading look at his mother.

"Along with the Cookie Monster Massacre of '99?" Stephanie couldn't resist teasing, delighting in the way Jack's ears turned pink.

"Sarah told you about that, didn't she?" He groaned. "I knew I should have bribed her with those chocolate croissants she loves."

Their playful banter was interrupted by Mayor Thompson's voice over the festival's PA system, announcing that the baking competition would begin in fifteen minutes. Stephanie felt her nerves return full force.

"Hey," Jack turned her to face him, his blue eyes serious. "You've got this. That cake is a masterpiece, just like everything you create."

"But what if—"

"No what-ifs," he said firmly. "Remember what you told me when I was nervous about performing surgery on Mr. Henderson's prize-winning horse? 'Trust your training, trust your heart, and everything else will follow.'"

Stephanie smiled, remembering that day. Jack had been pacing their apartment at dawn, reciting equine anatomy until she'd finally dragged him to the bakery and stress-baked cookies with him until sunrise. "When did you get so wise, Dr. Carter?"

"I learned from the best, Ms. Fields." He kissed her softly, then pulled back with a grin. "Now go show this town why I'm the luckiest man in Sweet Pine Valley."

With a deep breath, Stephanie headed toward the competition area. She could hear her parents and the Carters organizing themselves for prime viewing positions, and Sarah calling out last-minute good luck wishes. Tom had taken charge of Tessa, preparing her for the pet parade that would follow the baking competition.

The judges' table was impressive, featuring some of the region's most respected bakers and food critics. Stephanie recognized Margot Chen, owner of the prestigious White Mountain Culinary Institute, and James Patterson, food critic for the Burlington Free Press. But it was the third judge that made her pause – Helena Drake, her former mentor from her pastry school days in New York.

"Stephanie Fields," Helena's familiar voice carried across the square as Stephanie set up her cake. "I wondered if the rumors about you opening a small-town bakery were true."

"Helena," Stephanie managed a smile, though her hands trembled slightly as she made final adjustments to her display. "I didn't know you were judging today."

"Last-minute addition," Helena replied, her perfectly manicured fingers adjusting her designer glasses. "When I heard about this charming little festival, I simply had to see what kind of talent we might discover. Though I must admit, finding you here was... unexpected."

Before Stephanie could respond, Mayor Thompson began the competition introductions. She took her place among the other contestants, trying to focus on Jack's encouraging smile from the crowd rather than Helena's scrutinizing gaze.

One by one, the judges sampled each entry. Stephanie watched as they tasted Mrs. Henderson's classic apple pie, Clara's chocolate bourbon pecan tart, and several other impressive creations. Finally, they reached her cake.

"The construction is elegant," Margot Chen noted, examining the layers. "The temperature differential between the cake and frosting is perfectly maintained."

James Patterson took a bite, closing his eyes. "The flavor balance is exceptional. The pumpkin isn't overwhelmed by the spices, and the maple cream cheese frosting adds just the right amount of sweetness."

Then it was Helena's turn. Stephanie held her breath as her former mentor sampled the cake. Helena's expression remained neutral as she made notes on her scoring sheet, but Stephanie caught a slight raise of her eyebrows – the closest thing to approval she'd ever seen from the demanding chef.

The judges conferred quietly while the crowd buzzed with anticipation. Stephanie felt Jack's presence before she saw him, his hand finding hers and squeezing gently. Tessa had somehow escaped Tom's grasp and sat at their feet, her pilgrim hat slightly askew but her expression dignified.

"In third place," Mayor Thompson announced, "Clara's Coffee Corner with their chocolate bourbon pecan tart!"

The crowd applauded as Clara accepted her bronze ribbon, beaming with pride.

"In second place..." the Mayor paused dramatically, "Mrs. Henderson's heritage apple pie!"

More applause, and Mrs. Henderson wiped happy tears as she received her silver ribbon.

Stephanie's heart pounded. She felt Jack's arm slip around her waist, steady and supportive.

"And the grand prize winner of this year's Sweet Pine Valley Thanksgiving Festival Baking Competition..." Mayor Thompson opened the envelope with a flourish, "Fields of Sweet Dreams with their triple-layer pumpkin spice cake with maple cream cheese frosting and candied pecans!"

The square erupted in cheers. Stephanie stood frozen until Jack's kiss brought her back to reality. "You did it, sweetheart!" he whispered against her ear.

As she accepted the golden ribbon and small trophy, Stephanie caught Helena's eye. Her former mentor gave her a slight nod – high praise indeed from someone who had once told her she was throwing away her career by leaving New York.

The celebration was interrupted by the sounds of the pet parade organizing. Tom appeared to reclaim Tessa, who seemed more interested in the cake crumbs that had fallen near the judges' table.

"Go," Stephanie laughed, giving Jack a gentle push. "Get our little pilgrim ready for her debut. I'll pack up here."

As Jack and Tom led Tessa toward the parade staging area, Helena approached Stephanie's display.

"I admit," Helena said quietly, "when you left New York, I thought you were making a mistake. I couldn't understand why one of my most promising students would choose to open a small-town bakery when she could have been executive pastry chef at any restaurant in Manhattan."

Stephanie began carefully packing her cake carrier, considering her response. "I thought I was making a mistake too, at first," she admitted. "But then I realized that success isn't always measured in Michelin stars."

Helena's gaze drifted to where Jack was now helping to organize the pet parade participants, Tessa sitting proudly at his feet despite being the smallest dog present. "No," she said thoughtfully, "I suppose it isn't. Your technique has improved, by the way. There's a confidence in your baking that wasn't there before. Perhaps leaving New York wasn't such a mistake after all."

Before Stephanie could respond, the pet parade music began. She quickly finished packing up, not wanting to miss Tessa's moment in the spotlight. As she hurried toward the parade route, she heard Helena call after her.

"Stephanie? Save me a slice of wedding cake, won't you? I have a feeling it will be spectacular."

The pet parade was everything a small-town event should be – cheerfully chaotic and utterly charming. Tessa marched the entire route with her head held high, her pilgrim costume drawing coos from the crowd. Even when a large golden retriever dressed as a turkey gobbled too enthusiastically nearby, she maintained her composure, earning extra points from the judges for grace under pressure.

"Just like her mom," Jack whispered as they watched Tessa accept a participation ribbon, her tail wagging furiously.

The rest of the afternoon passed in a blur of festival activities. They sampled hot cider from Jack's father's booth, admired the children's thankful-thoughts paper turkey display, and helped Sarah sell handmade wreaths for the local animal shelter's fundraiser.

As twilight approached, the square's lights twinkled to life. Families gathered for the festival's closing ceremony, where Mayor Thompson would light the town's Christmas tree – Sweet Pine Valley's official transition from Thanksgiving to the Christmas season.

"Hard to believe it's been a year," Jack mused as they found a spot to watch the ceremony. Tessa, tired from her exciting day, dozed in Stephanie's arms, her pilgrim costume slightly rumpled.

"Since what?" Stephanie asked, though she already knew the answer.

"Since I first saw you standing right here, watching last year's tree lighting. You had flour in your hair and worry in your eyes, and all I could think was that I'd never seen anyone so beautiful."

"I was worried about the holiday rush," Stephanie remembered. "About proving to everyone – including myself – that I'd made the right choice coming here."

"And now?"

Stephanie looked around at their gathered families – her parents chatting with the Carters, Sarah and Tom sharing a thermos of hot chocolate, Helena deep in conversation with Margot Chen about possibly featuring Sweet Pine Valley in an upcoming food magazine. She felt Tessa's steady breathing against her chest and Jack's warm presence beside her.

"Now I know it wasn't just the right choice," she said softly. "It was the only choice. Everything that mattered was waiting for me here – I just didn't know it yet."

Jack's response was interrupted by Mayor Thompson beginning the countdown to the tree lighting. As the crowd chanted numbers, Stephanie felt Jack's arms wrap around her and Tessa, creating a perfect moment of belonging.

The tree blazed to life, its lights reflecting in the gently falling snow. Around them, the crowd oohed and aahed, but Stephanie barely noticed. She was too busy watching the lights dance in Jack's eyes as he looked at her with all the love in the world.

"Happy Thanksgiving, Stephanie Fields," he whispered.

"Happy Thanksgiving, Jack Carter," she replied, standing on tiptoe to kiss him as the first notes of "Silver Bells" filled the square.

Between them, Tessa stirred just enough to give a contented sigh, her pilgrim hat now completely askew but her heart, like theirs, perfectly at home.

Chapter 4

Unexpected News & Holiday Hopes

The Thanksgiving dinner table at Fields of Sweet Dreams looked like something out of a magazine spread. Stephanie and Marie had transformed the bakery's main room into an intimate dining space, with fall-colored linens, flickering candles, and arrangements of wheat stalks and autumn flowers. The extended families of both Fields and Carter clans filled every available seat, while Tessa, still wearing her now-rumpled pilgrim costume, made hopeful rounds beneath the table.

"Before we begin," Richard Carter stood, raising his glass, "I'd like to propose a toast. To our expanding family – to David and Lauren, who've given us the daughter we always wanted for Jack, to our Sarah and Tom for bringing us Tessa, and to Stephanie, who's not only won today's competition but has truly won all our hearts."

"Here, here!" The families raised their glasses, but Jack cleared his throat.

"Actually, Dad, if you don't mind, I have something to add." He stood, looking slightly nervous. Stephanie felt her heart skip – she recognized that expression. It was the same one he'd worn before proposing.

"As most of you know, I've been offered a partnership at Green Mountain Veterinary Hospital in Burlington," Jack began. A murmur went through the group. This was news to Stephanie, and she felt her mother's concerned gaze from across the table.

"What I haven't told anyone yet, except Stephanie," Jack continued, though this wasn't true – they hadn't discussed this at all, "is that I've decided to turn it down."

"Jack!" Marie gasped. "That's a prestigious position!"

"It is," he agreed, "but it would mean leaving Sweet Pine Valley. And instead, I've decided to buy Dr. Thompson's practice when he retires next month. He's agreed to stay on part-time to help with the transition."

The table erupted in excited chatter. Dr. Thompson had been Sweet Pine Valley's veterinarian for over forty years. His retirement had been the subject of worried speculation – many feared they'd be left without a local vet.

"But son," Richard leaned forward, "buying a practice... that's a significant investment."

"I know," Jack nodded. "Which brings me to my next announcement." He reached for Stephanie's hand. "The bank approved our loan this morning. We're buying not just the vet practice, but also the Victorian house on Maple Street. The one with the wraparound porch and the garden that Stephanie's been dreaming about."

Stephanie's free hand flew to her mouth. She knew exactly which house he meant – they'd walked past it countless times, admiring its gingerbread trim and imagining what it would be like to live there. But she'd had no idea Jack was planning this.

"The house needs some work," Jack admitted, "but it has space for a home office where I can do paperwork, a huge kitchen for Stephanie to test recipes, and..." he grinned, "a perfect spot for a Christmas tree in the front window. Plus, it's only two blocks from the bakery."

"Jack Carter," Stephanie finally found her voice, "are you telling me you bought us a house without telling me?"

The table went quiet, everyone holding their breath. Even Tessa stopped her rounds, sensing the tension.

"Actually," Jack's grin widened, "I'm asking you if you want to buy a house with me. The offer's been accepted, but I made sure it was contingent on your approval. I wouldn't make that decision without you, sweetheart."

Relief and joy bubbled up inside her. This was so typically Jack – romantic and thoughtful, but always respecting her independence. "And the vet practice?"

"Is my decision," he said firmly. "But I'm hoping you'll support it. Sweet Pine Valley is our home. I don't want to build our life anywhere else."

Stephanie stood, tears threatening to spill. "When can we see the house?"

"Tomorrow morning. Unless you'd rather wait—"

She cut him off with a kiss, prompting cheers and whistles from their families. Tessa, catching the excitement, gave a celebratory bark.

"Well," David Fields raised his glass again, "I guess we have even more to be thankful for than we thought."

The dinner that followed was filled with animated discussion about renovation plans, paint colors, and the future of both the veterinary practice and Fields of Sweet Dreams. Sarah and Tom offered to help with the move, while both sets of parents started planning how they could assist with the house renovations.

"The timing is perfect," Lauren Fields noted as she passed the sweet potatoes. "You can be settled in before Christmas."

"Speaking of Christmas," Marie added, "have you two set a wedding date yet?"

Stephanie and Jack exchanged glances. They'd been so busy with the bakery, Tessa's adoption, and the festival that wedding planning had taken a back seat.

"Actually," Stephanie said slowly, an idea forming, "what if we got married at Christmas? Not this year – it's too soon. But next Christmas, in the new house, once all the renovations are done?"

"A Christmas wedding!" Sarah clapped her hands. "It's perfect! We could decorate the whole house, have the ceremony in front of that big window Jack mentioned..."

"With snow falling outside," Jack added, warming to the idea. "And your famous hot chocolate for the reception..."

"And cookies instead of cake," Stephanie finished. It was just like them – finishing each other's thoughts, building on each other's dreams.

"Well," Helena spoke up from her end of the table, where she'd been quietly observing, "if you're having cookies instead of cake, you'll need someone to help coordinate the dessert menu. Someone with experience in large-scale pastry planning..."

Stephanie blinked in surprise. Was Helena offering to help with her wedding? The same Helena who'd once told her that leaving New York was career suicide?

"We'd be honored," Jack said smoothly, squeezing Stephanie's hand under the table. "Assuming you're willing to work with a small-town bakery."

Helena's lips twitched. "I think I can manage. Especially since your fiancée just proved she hasn't lost her touch." She raised her glass. "To new beginnings – in all their forms."

After dinner, as their families helped clear the tables and pack leftovers, Stephanie slipped outside onto the bakery's small back porch. The snow had stopped, leaving everything blanketed in pristine white. The festival lights still twinkled in the distance, and somewhere, someone was playing Christmas carols.

She heard the door open behind her and smiled, knowing it was Jack before he even spoke.

"Having second thoughts?" he asked softly, wrapping his arms around her from behind.

"About the house? Not a single one." She leaned back against him. "Though I am wondering how long you've been planning this."

"Remember last month when I had that emergency call about Mrs. Peterson's cat?" He chuckled. "The cat was fine. I was actually meeting with Dr. Thompson to discuss taking over the practice."

"Sneaky," she teased. "What else are you planning that I don't know about?"

"Well..." He turned her to face him. "There is one more thing. The house has a small cottage in the backyard. I was thinking... it would make a perfect studio apartment for Helena."

Stephanie's eyes widened. "What?"

"She mentioned at the festival that she's thinking of retiring from teaching. Said something about wanting to write a cookbook, maybe do some consulting. I thought... well, Sweet Pine Valley could use a culinary consultant. And you could use a mentor who's actually on your side this time."

"Jack..." Stephanie felt tears welling up again. "You'd do that? Even after how skeptical she was about small-town life?"

"I'd do anything to make you happy." He brushed a snowflake from her cheek. "Besides, I saw how she looked when she tasted your cake. That wasn't just approval – that was pride. She's already on your side, sweetheart. She just needed to see that you made the right choice."

Inside, they could hear their families laughing, the sounds of dishes clinking, and Tessa's nails clicking on the hardwood floors as she probably searched for dropped turkey bits. The festival lights painted the snow in rainbow colors, and the air smelled like woodsmoke and coming Christmas.

"I did, you know," Stephanie said softly. "Make the right choice. Every day, I choose this life. This town. You."

"Even with a house that needs renovating and a fiancé who springs major life changes on you at Thanksgiving dinner?"

"Especially then." She stood on tiptoe to kiss him. "Though next time you're planning to buy real estate, a little warning might be nice."

"Noted." He grinned. "Though I should warn you – I already have some ideas about Christmas decorations for the new house."

"Let me guess – inflatable Santa on the roof?"

"Please," he scoffed. "I was thinking more along the lines of a light-up reindeer family. To match our little family."

As if on cue, Tessa nosed open the back door, apparently having given up on finding more turkey scraps. She was still wearing her pilgrim collar, though the hat had long since disappeared.

"What do you think, girl?" Stephanie knelt down to scratch behind Tessa's ears. "Ready for a new adventure?"

Tessa's tail wagged enthusiastically, and she looked between them with complete trust in her eyes.

"I'll take that as a yes," Jack laughed. "Though we should probably warn her about the squirrels in that big oak tree in the backyard."

"And the fact that Helena might be her new neighbor?"

"Hey, you never know – Helena might turn out to be a dog person. Stranger things have happened." He pulled

Stephanie close again. "After all, a high-powered New York pastry chef fell in love with a small-town vet."

"And found everything she never knew she was looking for," Stephanie finished, resting her head on his chest.

Above them, the stars were coming out, bright and clear in the crisp November sky. The festival lights continued to twinkle, and somewhere in the distance, church bells began to chime. Between them, Tessa settled into a contented sit, her small body pressed against their legs as if to keep them together.

"Merry almost-Christmas," Jack whispered, his breath making clouds in the cold air.

"Merry almost-Christmas," Stephanie replied, knowing that this year's holiday season would be full of changes, challenges, and more love than she'd ever dreamed possible.

Behind them, the bakery door opened again, spilling warm light onto the snow. "Hey, lovebirds!" Sarah called. "Mom's breaking out the photo albums. Jack, if you want to prevent the Cookie Monster Massacre pictures from making an appearance, now's your chance!"

They laughed, turning to go back inside to their waiting families. But just for a moment longer, they stood in the gentle night, holding onto each other and this perfect moment of possibility.

The house on Maple Street waited for them, its wraparound porch and gingerbread trim promising new adventures. Dr. Thompson's practice stood ready for its next chapter. And somewhere in New York, Helena was perhaps already planning her own small-town transformation.

But for now, there was family, and laughter, and a little dachshund in a pilgrim costume. For now, there was the simple joy of being exactly where they were meant to be.

And that was more than enough.

Chapter 5

Home Sweet Home

The morning after Thanksgiving dawned clear and cold, with sunlight sparkling off the fresh snow like scattered diamonds. Stephanie stood at the bakery's apartment window, coffee in hand, watching the early risers of Sweet Pine Valley begin their day. The festival cleanup crew was already at work in the town square, dismantling booths and carefully storing decorations for next year.

"Ready for this?" Jack appeared behind her, already dressed for their house viewing. Tessa followed, wearing her warm winter sweater, her leash dangling from Jack's hand.

"I think so," Stephanie nodded, though butterflies danced in her stomach. "Is Helena still coming?"

After last night's revelation about the cottage, Helena had surprised everyone by expressing immediate interest in seeing the property. She'd even cancelled her return flight to New York to stay an extra day.

"She's meeting us there. Sarah and Tom are coming too – they insisted on lending their renovation expertise." Jack wrapped his arms around her waist. "Having second thoughts?"

"No," Stephanie said firmly. "Just first-time homeowner jitters. And maybe a few what-ifs about Helena actually moving here."

"Well, let's tackle one thing at a time." He kissed her temple. "First step: falling in love with our future home."

The house on Maple Street stood proud against the morning sky, its Victorian architecture enhanced by the fresh snow. The wraparound porch, though showing signs of wear, maintained its elegant charm. Window boxes, now empty for winter, hinted at spring possibilities.

"Oh, Jack," Stephanie breathed as they approached. "It's even more beautiful up close."

Sarah and Tom were already waiting on the porch steps, armed with notepads and measuring tape. Helena stood slightly apart, studying the property with an appraising eye.

"The cottage has good bones," she remarked as they approached. "Though it will need considerable updating."

"Starting to reconsider small-town life?" Jack asked carefully.

Helena's lips curved slightly. "On the contrary. I'm wondering why I didn't think of it sooner. Sometimes you need a former student to show you new possibilities."

Before Stephanie could respond, the real estate agent arrived – none other than Mrs. Henderson from the hardware store, who also happened to be Sweet Pine Valley's most successful realtor.

"Good morning, everyone!" She beamed, keys jingling. "Ready to see your future home?"

The front door opened to reveal a spacious entryway with original hardwood floors and a curved staircase. Despite the house being empty, sunshine streamed through the large windows, creating warm pools of light on the floor.

"The previous owners maintained the historical features," Mrs. Henderson explained as they moved through the rooms. "All the original woodwork, the pocket doors between the parlor and dining room, even the stained glass window on the landing."

Stephanie could already envision their life here. The formal dining room would be perfect for family gatherings. The living room's bay window – exactly where Jack had mentioned – would frame their Christmas tree perfectly. The kitchen, though outdated, was spacious enough for her to test recipes and perhaps even film the baking tutorials her followers had been requesting.

"The appliances all need updating," Tom noted, examining the kitchen. "But the layout is solid. We could add an island here, maybe some open shelving along this wall..."

"And look at these built-in cabinets!" Sarah ran her hand along the original glass-fronted hutch. "Just imagine displaying all your grandmother's china here, Jack."

While the others discussed renovation possibilities, Stephanie noticed Tessa had disappeared. She found the little dachshund in what would be the master bedroom, sitting in a patch of sunlight streaming through the large windows that overlooked the backyard.

"Found your spot already, sweet girl?" Stephanie knelt beside her. Through the window, she could see the cottage where Helena might live, the large oak tree Jack had mentioned, and beyond that, a view of the mountains that made Sweet Pine Valley famous.

"She has good taste," Helena's voice came from the doorway. "This room has excellent natural light. Perfect for photography – say, for a cookbook?"

Stephanie turned, surprised. "You're really serious about the cookbook?"

"I'm serious about many things," Helena moved to stand beside her. "Including admitting when I've been wrong. I thought success could only look one way – my way. But yesterday, watching you in that competition, seeing how you've built not just a business but a life here... it made me realize I've been measuring success with the wrong metrics."

"So you're really considering the cottage?"

"More than considering. I called my lawyer this morning. I'm preparing an offer." Helena's usual crisp tone softened. "That is if you and Jack are comfortable having your former mentor as a neighbor."

"Are you kidding?" Stephanie stood, impulsively hugging Helena. "Having you here would be amazing! You could help with the wedding planning, and the cookbook... wait, is that why you want the natural light? Are you thinking of featuring local recipes?"

"Among other things." Helena adjusted her glasses, but Stephanie caught the smile in her eyes. "Sweet Pine Valley's Fields of Sweet Dreams has been garnering quite a bit of attention in certain circles. Especially after yesterday's festival. It might be time for the culinary world to discover what small-town baking is really about."

From downstairs, they heard Jack calling. They found him in the kitchen with Mrs. Henderson, Sarah, and Tom, all gathered around what looked like preliminary renovation plans Tom had already sketched.

"So," Jack asked as Stephanie joined them, "what do you think? Should we make an offer?"

Stephanie looked around at the kitchen that needed updating but had so much potential, through the doorway to the dining room where she could already imagine holiday gatherings, past the stairs that led to sun-filled bedrooms and the window seat where she'd found Tessa.

"Actually," Mrs. Henderson interjected with a smile, "that's why I asked you all here today specifically. The sellers received your offer last night, Jack. They've accepted."

"What?" Stephanie turned to Jack. "But you said—"

"I said the offer was contingent on your approval," he grinned. "I never said I hadn't made one. But we can still walk away if you don't love it."

"Walk away?" Stephanie laughed, tears springing to her eyes. "Jack Carter, this is perfect. It's exactly what we need. Though we're going to have a serious discussion about your tendency to spring life-changing surprises on me."

"Speaking of surprises," Helena cleared her throat, "perhaps this is a good time to mention that I've already spoken with the sellers about the cottage. They've agreed to sell it separately. It seems Sweet Pine Valley is about to gain another resident."

The kitchen erupted in excited chatter. Sarah immediately began talking about welcoming Helena to the neighborhood, while Tom launched into his renovation ideas for both properties. Through it all, Tessa pranced around their feet, seeming to sense the joy in the room.

"There is one more thing," Jack said when the excitement died down. He reached into his pocket and pulled out what looked like an old brass key. "Mrs. Henderson found this in the attic. Apparently, it's the original key to the front door from when the house was built in 1892. I thought maybe we could use it in our Christmas wedding next year – you know, symbolically starting our new chapter in this historic home."

Stephanie took the key, feeling its weight in her hand. "You really have thought of everything, haven't you?"

"I tried." He pulled her close. "Though I'm sure there are plenty of surprises still ahead. Renovations have a way of throwing curveballs."

"Speaking of which," Tom interrupted, spreading his sketches on the counter, "we should talk about timeline. If you want to be in by Christmas this year and have the wedding here next Christmas, we need to prioritize certain projects."

The next hour was spent planning. Tom, who had renovated several historic homes, outlined the most critical updates needed. Sarah, with her interior design background, suggested ways to maintain the house's character while modernizing its functionality. Helena offered insights about kitchen layout based on her years of professional experience.

As they talked, Stephanie found herself wandering through the rooms again, this time really seeing their future unfold. The wall where their family photos would hang. The corner where Tessa's bed would go. The window seat that would become her favorite reading spot.

She found Jack in what would be their home office, staring out at the view of downtown Sweet Pine Valley, the bakery's sign just visible in the distance.

"Penny for your thoughts?" she asked, slipping her arm around his waist.

"Just thinking about how far we've come," he replied. "A year ago, you were wondering if moving here was a mistake, and I was trying to figure out how to ask out the beautiful baker who'd stolen my heart. Now look at us – engaged, homeowners, with a growing family that includes a former New York culinary icon and a dachshund in designer sweaters."

"Speaking of family," Stephanie hesitated, "there's something we should probably discuss. That extra bedroom down the hall..."

Jack turned to face her, his eyes softening. "The one with the perfect morning light and built-in bookshelves?"

"I was thinking it might make a nice nursery. You know, someday. Not right away, but..."

"Someday," he agreed, pulling her close. "Though we might want to wait until after we've survived the renovations. And the wedding planning. And Helena moving in next door."

"And the cookbook project she's obviously planning."

"And teaching Tessa to coexist with the backyard squirrels."

They laughed together, the sound echoing through their future home. From downstairs, they could hear Sarah and Tom debating paint colors, while Helena's voice carried something about proper kitchen ventilation systems.

"We should probably get back down there," Stephanie sighed. "Before they plan our entire renovation without us."

"One minute more," Jack murmured, holding her close. "I just want to remember this moment. Standing in our future home, planning our future family, with all our dreams ahead of us."

"Even if those dreams include Helena critiquing our kitchen equipment?"

"Even then." He kissed her softly. "Besides, having a world-renowned chef as a neighbor might come in handy. Especially when we're too tired from renovating to cook."

"Jack! Stephanie!" Sarah's voice carried up the stairs. "Tom's found original blueprints in the basement!"

They shared one more kiss before heading downstairs to join their renovation crew. Tessa met them at the bottom of the stairs, her tail wagging as if she already knew this was home.

The rest of the morning passed in a whirlwind of planning and dreaming. By the time they left, Tom had a preliminary renovation schedule drawn up, Sarah had color schemes planned for each room, and Helena had detailed specifications for both kitchen renovations – the main house and the cottage.

Standing on the porch for one last look, Stephanie felt Jack's arms wrap around her from behind.

"Welcome home, almost-Mrs. Carter," he whispered.

"Welcome home, Mr. Carter," she replied, leaning back against him. "Think we're ready for this adventure?"

As if in answer, Tessa barked once, her sound echoing across their new front yard. Above them, a pair of cardinals – Christmas birds, Stephanie's grandmother would have called them – landed on the porch railing.

"I'd say that's a yes," Jack chuckled. "Though maybe we should stock up on coffee and patience before the renovations begin."

"And dog treats," Stephanie added, watching Tessa eye the squirrel now perched in their oak tree. "Lots of dog treats."

They walked back to the bakery hand in hand, their feet leaving tracks in the fresh snow, while Helena headed to the real estate office to make her offer on the cottage. The morning sun had melted some of the festival decorations' frost, making them sparkle like prisms.

Sweet Pine Valley was waking up to another beautiful day, unaware that its story was about to gain new chapters – a restored Victorian, a renowned chef, and a family whose journey was just beginning.

And in Stephanie's pocket, an antique brass key waited to unlock their future.

Chapter 6

Snowflakes and Surprises

December arrived in Sweet Pine Valley with a flurry of snowflakes and the sound of hammers. The Victorian house on Maple Street hummed with activity as Tom's renovation crew tackled the first phase of updates. The kitchen had been completely gutted, the master bathroom was down to the studs, and somewhere beneath a mountain of drop cloths, their dream home was slowly taking shape.

"Watch your step!" Tom called as Stephanie navigated her way through the construction zone, carrying two cardboard trays of coffee and a box of fresh pastries from the bakery. "We just removed some floorboards in the hallway."

"I noticed," she laughed, carefully sidestepping the gap. "Though I think the real challenge will be keeping Tessa from treating it like an obstacle course."

As if on cue, their little dachshund attempted to follow her path, only to be scooped up by Jack as he came down the stairs.

"Not today, adventurer," he told the squirming pup. "Though I have to admit, she's getting braver by the day. This morning she actually barked at the demolition noise instead of hiding under the bed."

"Speaking of brave," Tom accepted a coffee gratefully, "Helena's cottage renovation is moving faster than expected. The crew over there found fewer issues than we anticipated."

"That's because Helena plans everything down to the last detail," Stephanie smiled, thinking of the thirty-page renovation document her former mentor had presented to the contractors. "Though I still can't believe she's really moving here. She called this morning to ask about local farmer's markets for the cookbook research."

"The cookbook that you're co-authoring," Jack reminded her proudly. "Don't forget that part."

The cookbook had been Helena's idea, proposed over dinner two nights ago. "Sweet Pine Valley Seasons" would feature both traditional and innovative recipes, telling the story of small-town baking through the changing calendar. Helena had already secured a publisher, arguing that the timing was perfect – a celebrated New York chef embracing small-town life was apparently a compelling narrative.

"Speaking of not forgetting things," Tom interrupted, checking his phone, "Sarah's messaging about the Christmas window display at the bakery. Something about Helena offering to help?"

"Oh!" Stephanie checked her watch. "I almost forgot! Helena wanted to see how we do small-town Christmas. She's probably already at the bakery, wondering where I am."

"Go," Jack kissed her quickly. "I'll handle things here. Though maybe take Tessa with you? She's been eyeing that hole in the floor a little too enthusiastically."

The walk to Fields of Sweet Dreams was like strolling through a Christmas card. The town's holiday decorations were up in full force – garlands and red ribbons adorned every lamppost, and the shop windows sparkled with festive displays.

Even the morning air seemed to hold a hint of pine and cinnamon.

"There you are!" Sarah called from the bakery's doorway. "Helena's been reorganizing your supply closet for the past twenty minutes. I think she's stress-cleaning."

Sure enough, they found Helena amid a perfectly arranged collection of cake pans and piping tips, her designer outfit somehow remaining immaculate despite the dusty shelves.

"Your inventory system needed updating," she said by way of greeting. "Especially if we're going to be testing recipes for the book. Now, about this window display – Sarah tells me it's something of a town tradition?"

"The Christmas window competition," Stephanie nodded, unleashing Tessa who immediately went to investigate the supply closet's new organization. "Every business creates a holiday display. The winner gets their business featured in the town's Christmas Eve parade."

"And Fields of Sweet Dreams has never won," Sarah added. "Though not for lack of trying. Last year's gingerbread village was beautiful."

"Until that unfortunate humidity issue," Stephanie remembered with a grimace. "Who knew gingerbread could melt quite like that?"

"Well," Helena straightened her blazer, "this year will be different. I've been thinking about a concept that combines traditional small-town charm with modern execution. Picture this: a winter wonderland made entirely of pulled sugar and isomalt, with blown sugar ornaments catching the light..."

As Helena outlined her vision, Stephanie felt a familiar mix of awe and anxiety. The design was ambitious – possibly too ambitious for their small bakery's resources. But before she could voice her concerns, the bell above the door chimed.

"Special delivery!" Jack's voice rang out. He entered carrying what appeared to be several large boxes, followed by Tom with even more. "Found these in the house's attic. The previous owners said we could keep them."

"Christmas decorations?" Sarah peered into one of the boxes. "Oh my goodness, these are gorgeous! Look at these vintage ornaments!"

The boxes contained a treasure trove of holiday decorations from various eras – delicate glass ornaments, hand-painted ceramic figures, and even a collection of antique cookie cutters.

"These are museum-quality pieces," Helena marveled, carefully lifting a hand-blown glass snowflake. "And look – the date on this box says 1892. These must be original to the house."

Stephanie picked up one of the cookie cutters, its design still crisp after all these years. "These were made for professional use. See the reinforced edges? These came from a real bakery."

"Actually," Jack pulled out an old photograph he'd found at the bottom of a box, "I think they came from your bakery."

The sepia-toned image showed Fields of Sweet Dreams circa 1892, its window display featuring an elaborate Christmas scene made of cookies and candies. The baker, a woman in a long dress and apron, stood proudly in the doorway.

"That's Elizabeth Fields," Mrs. Henderson's voice made them all jump. She'd entered unnoticed during their exploration. "The original owner of Fields of Sweet Dreams. And if I'm not mistaken, those are her cookie cutters you're holding, Stephanie."

"But... my last name is Fields, but I'm not..."

"Related?" Mrs. Henderson smiled. "Actually, dear, you are. Very distantly, through your father's mother's side. Why do you think the bank was so willing to give you the loan for the bakery two years ago? They loved the idea of a Fields returning to Fields of Sweet Dreams."

Stephanie sank onto a nearby chair, stunned. "You knew? All this time?"

"I suspected when you first arrived," Mrs. Henderson admitted. "Then I confirmed it when you applied for the loan. I thought you knew – it's all in the property records."

"So when Jack and I bought the Victorian..." Stephanie looked at the photograph again.

"Elizabeth Fields lived there too," Mrs. Henderson nodded. "She built both the house and the bakery. The cottage was originally her mother's home."

Helena picked up the glass snowflake again, examining it thoughtfully. "Well, it seems the universe has a sense of poetry. A Fields returns to the bakery, the house, and now the cottage will house a baker again. Though I doubt Elizabeth Fields ever imagined a New York chef would be moving in."

"Wait," Sarah grabbed the photograph for a closer look. "The window display in this picture – it's exactly like what Helena was just describing! A winter wonderland made of cookies and candy!"

"That settles it then," Helena declared. "We'll recreate Elizabeth's display, but with modern techniques. A blend of past and present, just like Fields of Sweet Dreams itself."

The rest of the morning was spent unpacking the Christmas decorations and planning the window display. Helena sketched designs while Sarah cataloged the vintage ornaments. Tessa supervised from her new favorite spot near the register, occasionally offering supportive woofs when someone seemed particularly excited.

Jack had to return to the house to meet with the electrician, but not before pulling Stephanie aside. "You okay? That was quite a revelation about Elizabeth Fields."

"I'm..." she paused, considering. "I'm overwhelmed, but in a good way. It's like finding a missing puzzle piece I didn't know was missing. All this time I've felt drawn to this place, to this life, and now I know why. It's literally in my blood."

"Blood and sugar," he teased, kissing her forehead. "Speaking of which, don't let Helena go too crazy with the display. We still need you in one piece for Christmas."

But Helena's enthusiasm was contagious. As they worked, she shared stories of her own early days in New York, learning to work with sugar and chocolate from old-world masters. "They taught me that baking isn't just about recipes – it's about legacy. About passing down not just techniques, but love."

"Like Elizabeth passing down her cookie cutters without even knowing it," Stephanie mused, running her finger along one of the antique cutters. "I wonder what she'd think of all this."

"I think," Mrs. Henderson said softly, "she'd be very proud. Not just of the bakery's success, but of how you've made it a heart of the community again. That was always her dream – to create a place where sweetness wasn't just about sugar."

By lunchtime, they had a solid plan for the window display. Helena's modern sugar techniques would recreate Elizabeth's original design, incorporating some of the vintage decorations. Sarah had already started calculating lighting angles to best showcase the sugar work.

"We'll need to start the sugar pieces tomorrow," Helena announced, checking her ever-present notebook. "The humidity forecast looks favorable for the next week. Stephanie, I assume you've worked with isomalt before?"

"In pastry school," Stephanie nodded. "Though not on this scale."

"Perfect time to learn more," Helena smiled. "Consider it research for the cookbook's advanced techniques chapter."

As if the day hadn't held enough surprises, Jack returned with news from the house. "The electrician found something interesting behind one of the walls – a collection of old letters. They're addressed to Elizabeth Fields."

That evening, after the bakery closed, Stephanie sat in the apartment above Fields of Sweet Dreams, carefully reading through Elizabeth's letters. They told a story of determination, of a woman who refused to be limited by her era's expectations. She'd built not just a bakery and a house, but a legacy.

"Listen to this," she read aloud to Jack, who was attempting to untangle a string of vintage Christmas lights while Tessa "helped" by pouncing on the wire. "'My mother says a woman has no business owning property, but I believe we must follow our hearts, even when the path proves difficult. The house is nearly complete, and the bakery's Christmas display is the talk of the town. Perhaps in years to come, another baker will stand in this window, creating their own magic.'"

"Sounds like someone else I know," Jack smiled. "A certain baker who took a chance on a small town and created her own magic."

"We both did," Stephanie set down the letters and moved to help him with the lights. "Though I have to admit, learning about Elizabeth makes me feel even more pressure about the window display. We're not just competing for the parade now – we're carrying on her legacy."

"You'll do her proud," Jack assured her. "Besides, you have something Elizabeth didn't."

"What's that?"

"A world-famous chef as your sugar-work assistant," he grinned. "Though I'm a little worried Helena might try to add a scale model of the New York skyline made of pulled sugar."

"Actually," Stephanie laughed, "she's fully embraced the small-town aesthetic. This morning she was asking about the possibility of keeping chickens at the cottage."

They worked in comfortable silence for a while, untangling lights and reading more letters. Tessa eventually gave up on "helping" and curled up in her bed, though she kept one eye on them as if making sure they were doing it right.

"You know what else Elizabeth had?" Jack said suddenly. "A complete family and deep roots in the community. Her letters mention Sunday dinners, holiday gatherings, generations of recipes passed down. And now, a hundred and thirty years later, her legacy helped bring us together. The bakery, the house, even Helena moving here – it's all connected."

"Like it was meant to be," Stephanie agreed. She picked up the glass snowflake they'd found earlier, watching it catch the light. "Do you think we'll leave a legacy like that? Something that will touch lives a hundred years from now?"

"I think," Jack pulled her close, "we already are. Every day, with every cookie you bake, every animal I help, every life we touch – we're building our chapter of the story. And now we know it's part of a much bigger story."

Outside, snow began to fall again, soft and steady. The vintage lights, finally untangled, cast a warm glow around the apartment. From her bed, Tessa sighed contentedly.

Tomorrow would bring sugar-work with Helena, more renovation challenges, and all the busy joy of the holiday season. But for now, Stephanie was content to sit with Jack, surrounded by pieces of Elizabeth Fields' life, and dream about their own legacy in the making.

After all, as Elizabeth had written in one of her letters: "A home, like a life well-lived, is built one day at a time, with equal measures of love, courage, and just a sprinkling of sugar."

Chapter 7

Sugar and Snowstorms

"Hold that isomalt steady," Helena instructed, her usual commanding tone softened by concentration. "We need absolute precision for this piece."

Stephanie carefully maintained her grip on the delicate sugar structure that would become the centerpiece of their Christmas window display. After three days of intensive work, Elizabeth Fields' original design was slowly coming to life in a stunning combination of old and new techniques.

"Perfect," Helena nodded as the final spun-sugar icicle was attached. "Now we just need the vintage ornaments Sarah promised to bring—"

The bakery door burst open, letting in a swirl of snow and a very windblown Sarah.

"We have a problem," she announced, stamping snow from her boots. "The weather service just issued a severe winter storm warning. We're looking at two feet of snow in the next twenty-four hours."

Stephanie and Helena exchanged alarmed looks. Isomalt work was finicky enough in perfect conditions – a major storm could spell disaster for their delicate creation.

"What about the humidity?" Stephanie asked, already reaching for her phone to check the forecast.

"That's not our only problem," Sarah continued. "The storm is threatening to cancel the Christmas parade. The town council's meeting right now to decide."

"But the window display competition—" Stephanie began.

"Will still happen," Jack's voice came from the doorway. He entered with Tessa, both covered in snow. "Just spoke with Mayor Thompson. They're moving everything up. Judging will be tonight, before the storm hits."

"Tonight?" Helena's usually unflappable demeanor cracked slightly. "But we're not finished! We still need the lighting effects Sarah designed, and the sugar ribbon work for the border—"

"Then we better work fast," Stephanie said firmly, channeling both Elizabeth Fields' determination and Helena's efficiency. "Sarah, can you get the lights set up now? Jack, we'll need more hands for the sugar work. How are your pulling techniques?"

"Rusty but willing," he grinned, shrugging off his coat. "Tom's securing things at the house, but he'll be here soon to help too. Though I should warn you – the storm's already picking up."

The next few hours were a blur of activity. Helena proved to be an unexpectedly patient teacher as she guided Jack through basic sugar-pulling techniques. Sarah worked magic with the lighting, incorporating some of the vintage Christmas lights they'd found in Elizabeth's boxes. Tessa appointed herself quality control supervisor, maintaining a dignified watch from beneath the worktable.

"The temperature's dropping fast," Tom reported when he arrived, bringing with him the last of the vintage ornaments they'd carefully cleaned. "But you should see the house – we got the new windows installed just in time. Your view of downtown will be perfect for watching the storm roll in."

"Assuming we make it there tonight," Jack said, carefully placing a sugar snowflake into position. "The roads are getting bad."

"We'll make it," Stephanie said with more confidence than she felt. "Elizabeth didn't let anything stop her from creating Christmas magic, and neither will we."

As if in response to her words, they heard a crack of thunder – highly unusual for a December storm.

"Thundersnow," Helena mused, adjusting a spun-sugar icicle. "I haven't seen that since my first winter in New York. The year I won my first pastry competition, actually. I always considered it good luck."

The window display was coming together beautifully. Delicate sugar sculptures caught and reflected light from the vintage bulbs, creating an ethereal glow. The antique ornaments added touches of color and history, while pulled-sugar ribbons seemed to dance around the entire creation. At the center, a perfect recreation of Fields of Sweet Dreams circa 1892 stood in miniature, crafted from isomalt and edible paint.

"Elizabeth would be proud," Mrs. Henderson's voice made them all turn. She stood in the doorway, snow dusting her shoulders. "The judges are making their rounds early because of the storm. They'll be here in twenty minutes."

Twenty minutes. Stephanie looked at their creation – so close to finished, yet still missing crucial elements. The sugar ribbon border wasn't complete, and they hadn't had time to add the final dusting of edible shimmer that would make the whole thing sparkle like fresh snow.

"Right," Helena straightened her spine, every inch the acclaimed chef who had taught Stephanie to never accept anything less than perfection. "Sarah, adjust the blue light three degrees to the left. Tom, we need that ladder positioned exactly below the last gap in the border. Jack, your sugar-pulling technique has improved remarkably – think you can manage one more ribbon?"

They worked with focused intensity as the storm grew stronger outside. Tessa abandoned her supervisory position to press against the door, whining softly at the thunder.

"Almost there," Stephanie murmured, carefully applying the last touches of shimmer powder. Through the window, she could see the judges making their way down the street, huddled against the wind.

"Wait!" Sarah called from the ladder. "One last thing." She reached into her bag and pulled out what appeared to be one of Elizabeth's original cookie cutters, polished to a soft gleam. "We should add this – right here, where everyone can see it."

The judges entered just as Sarah was climbing down from positioning the cookie cutter. Outside, the storm had turned the afternoon dark enough that their lights created an almost magical glow in the dimness.

Margot Chen from the culinary institute was among the judges again. She studied the display with professional interest, occasionally making notes. James Patterson circled it twice, pausing to examine the sugar work closely.

"The technical skill is impressive," he murmured. "This ribbon work – it's reminiscent of Dubois' style, but with a modern twist."

"That would be my influence," Helena said quietly. "Though the design is pure Sweet Pine Valley, inspired by Elizabeth Fields herself."

The judges conferred in low voices while everyone tried not to hover anxiously. Tessa, perhaps sensing the tension, pressed against Stephanie's legs supportively.

Finally, Margot turned to address them. "We still have two more displays to judge, but given the weather, I feel comfortable saying this: in all my years of judging food competitions, I've never seen such a perfect blend of technical expertise and emotional resonance. The way you've honored history while showcasing modern skill is remarkable."

They barely had time to process this encouraging feedback before the judges hurried out into the increasingly treacherous weather.

"Well," Jack wrapped an arm around Stephanie's waist, "I'd say that went well. Though I'm more concerned about getting everyone home safely before this storm gets worse."

As if underlining his point, another crack of thunder shook the windows.

"The cottage is almost finished," Helena mused, watching the snow swirl outside. "But perhaps not quite ready for tonight."

"You'll stay with us," Stephanie said firmly. "We can all stay at the apartment tonight. It'll be cozy, but it's better than trying to drive in this."

The next hour was spent preparing for what looked to be an impromptu slumber party. Sarah and Tom ran home to grab essentials and their emergency overnight bags (a necessity in Vermont winters), while Jack and Stephanie gathered every spare blanket they owned.

Helena, ever practical, took charge of dinner preparations. "I found some homemade soup in your freezer," she called from the kitchen. "And with a little help, I think we can manage enough fresh bread to go with it."

The bread-baking lesson that followed was unlike any Stephanie had experienced in culinary school. Helena was more relaxed, sharing stories of her own early days learning to bake in her grandmother's kitchen.

"I forgot, sometimes," she admitted as she demonstrated the perfect kneading technique, "that before all the acclaim and awards, baking was simply about bringing comfort and joy. It took coming here to remember that."

The storm grew fiercer as evening fell, but inside Fields of Sweet Dreams, all was warm and cozy. Sarah and Tom returned with not just overnight supplies but also board games and hot chocolate fixings. Jack built a fire in the apartment's small fireplace, while Tessa made sure everyone had settled in their proper places – primarily by claiming a spot on each person's lap in rotation.

"The judges just posted their decision online," Sarah announced around eight o'clock, checking her phone. "They finished early because of the storm."

Everyone fell silent, waiting.

Sarah's face broke into a huge grin. "We won! Fields of Sweet Dreams takes first place! Listen to this – 'A masterpiece of technical skill and historical significance, this display represents everything that makes Small Pine Valley special. The judges were particularly moved by the incorporation of original elements from the bakery's founding days, including an antique cookie cutter that once belonged to Elizabeth Fields herself.'"

The celebration that followed was made even sweeter by the howling storm outside. They toasted with hot chocolate (enhanced with a touch of peppermint schnapps that Tom produced from his emergency supplies), and Helena actually unbent enough to join in when Sarah suggested charades.

Later, as everyone settled in for the night – Sarah and Tom on the pull-out couch, Helena surprisingly content on the oversized armchair, Jack and Stephanie in their bed with Tessa snuggled between them – Stephanie found herself thinking about legacy again.

"What's on your mind?" Jack whispered, noticing she was still awake.

"Just thinking about Elizabeth," she whispered back. "About how she probably had nights like this too – stuck in a storm, but surrounded by people she cared about. Making the best of things, creating memories."

"Speaking of memories," Jack propped himself up on one elbow, "I have something for you. I was going to wait until Christmas, but..." He reached carefully over Tessa to retrieve something from his bedside drawer.

It was a small album, clearly antique but well-preserved.

"I found it at the house today, just before the storm hit," he explained as Stephanie carefully opened it. "It's Elizabeth's personal photo album. Look at the first page."

There, in a photo yellowed with age, was their living room – decorated for Christmas in 1892. The tree stood exactly where they planned to put theirs, and hanging from the mantel were stockings that looked remarkably like the ones they'd found in the attic.

"Turn to the last page," Jack suggested softly.

The final photo showed Elizabeth in her later years, surrounded by family, standing proudly in front of Fields of Sweet Dreams. Written beneath in careful script were the words: "Remember always that a home is built of love, a business of dedication, and a life of both. May future generations find their own way to keep the sweetness alive."

Stephanie felt tears welling up. "It's like she knew," she whispered. "Like she was leaving these things for us to find, piece by piece."

"Maybe she did know," Jack mused. "Maybe she had faith that someday, the right person would come along to carry on her legacy. Though I doubt even Elizabeth could have predicted that legacy would include a renowned New York chef sleeping in an armchair while a thundersnow rages outside."

From the living room, they heard a quiet laugh – Helena, apparently not quite asleep, had heard them. "I'll have you know," she called softly, "that this armchair is more comfortable than my thousand-dollar ergonomic desk chair in New York."

"Shh," Sarah's sleepy voice joined in. "Some of us are trying to dream about our window display victory."

"Some of us," Tom added, "are trying to dream about not having to shovel two feet of snow tomorrow."

Tessa, disturbed by all the chattering, gave a dramatic sigh and rearranged herself against Stephanie's side.

Outside, the storm continued its bluster, but inside, wrapped in the warmth of friendship and history, everything was perfect. As Stephanie drifted off to sleep, she could almost imagine Elizabeth Fields looking down on them all, pleased to see her beloved home and bakery filled with so much love and laughter.

Tomorrow would bring shoveling and storm cleanup, more renovation challenges, and all the busy joy of the holiday season. But tonight, in this cozy haven they'd created, Stephanie knew with absolute certainty that she was exactly where she was meant to be – carrying on a legacy of love, sugar, and the simple magic of bringing people together.

Chapter 8

After the Storm

Morning arrived with a hushed stillness that only follows a major snowstorm. Stephanie woke to find Tessa already at the apartment window, her nose pressed against the glass as she surveyed a world transformed. Sweet Pine Valley lay under a thick blanket of pristine white, the storm having dropped even more snow than predicted.

"It's beautiful," Jack murmured, joining them at the window. "Though I'm a little worried about the house. That's a lot of snow on the temporary roof covers."

From the living room came the sounds of their overnight guests stirring. Helena, surprisingly cheerful for someone who'd spent the night in an armchair, was already in the kitchen making coffee. Sarah and Tom were folding up their makeshift bed, while discussing the best snow-removal strategy.

"The bakery's window display!" Stephanie suddenly remembered. "We need to check if it survived the storm!"

They hurried downstairs, Tessa bouncing through snow drifts that nearly topped her head. The display window, when they reached it, was intact – and more magical than ever. The morning sun caught each sugar sculpture perfectly, creating rainbow prisms that danced across the fresh snow. The vintage ornaments glowed warmly, and Elizabeth's cookie cutter held pride of place, telling its century-old story to a new generation.

"It's a Christmas miracle," Sarah breathed, joining them outside. "Everything survived intact."

"Not quite everything," Tom's voice came from around the corner. "You better come see this."

They found him staring up at the Victorian house. The temporary covering over the partially finished roof had partially collapsed under the snow's weight, and water was visibly dripping into the upper floor.

"No, no, no," Jack muttered, already pulling out his phone to call the contractors. "We can't have water damage now. Not when we're so close to being done."

"The forecast shows another storm coming in three days," Tom reported, checking his weather app. "We need to get this fixed fast."

"The cottage," Helena spoke up. She'd followed them, wrapped in what appeared to be one of Stephanie's spare coats. "It's finished enough to be livable. Why don't you all stay there while the repairs are made? I can delay my move for a few weeks."

"We couldn't possibly—" Stephanie began, but Helena held up a hand.

"Consider it a Christmas gift. Besides, I'm still officially living in New York until after the holidays. The cottage has heat, running water, and a functioning kitchen. It's the logical solution."

Before anyone could respond, Mrs. Henderson came hurrying up the street, somehow managing to look elegant despite navigating through knee-deep snow.

"Emergency town council meeting in an hour," she announced. "The storm damaged the community center's roof.

They're looking for alternate locations for the annual Christmas charity dinner."

The Christmas charity dinner was a Sweet Pine Valley tradition, providing a holiday meal and gifts for families in need. Last year, they'd served over two hundred people.

"They can use the bakery," Stephanie said immediately. "We have the space, especially if we move some display cases."

"The bakery that's already preparing for the holiday rush?" Helena raised an eyebrow. "While you're dealing with house repairs and living in temporary quarters?"

"Elizabeth would have done it," Stephanie said simply.

Helena's expression softened. "Yes, I suppose she would have. Well then, we better get organized. Sarah, we'll need to reconfigure the bakery layout. Tom, can your crew spare someone to help move furniture? Jack, you handle the house situation. Stephanie..." she paused, a small smile playing at her lips, "you and I have a Christmas dinner for two hundred to plan."

The next few hours passed in a whirlwind of activity. The town's snow removal crews had the main streets cleared by mid-morning, allowing Tom's construction team to access the house. The damage, while concerning, was repairable – but it would take at least two weeks.

Meanwhile, the bakery transformed. Display cases were rearranged to create seating space, keeping the window display safely protected. Sarah's interior design skills proved invaluable as she figured out how to maximize the space while maintaining its charm.

"We could use these," she said, pulling out a box of Elizabeth's vintage Christmas decorations. "Create little centerpieces for each table with the older, sturdier pieces."

Helena, in her element, had commandeered the kitchen. She and Stephanie worked side by side, planning a menu that would be both festive and practical for large-scale preparation. Tessa supervised from her new favorite spot near the ovens, occasionally offering encouraging woofs when particularly good ideas were proposed.

"We'll need volunteers," Stephanie realized, looking at their growing list of tasks. "Especially since we'll still be handling regular bakery orders."

"Already handled," Mrs. Henderson appeared with a clipboard. "Half the town has signed up to help. The high school's home economics class wants to make cookies, the garden club is handling decorations, and the local restaurants are all offering to prepare side dishes."

"See?" Jack squeezed Stephanie's shoulders as he came in from checking on the house repairs. "This is what small towns do – we come together."

"Speaking of coming together," Helena interjected, "we should discuss sleeping arrangements. The cottage has two bedrooms. I suggest Stephanie and Jack take the master, and Sarah and Tom take the second room. I'll stay in the apartment above the bakery – it'll be more convenient for early morning baking anyway."

"But—" Stephanie started to protest.

"No arguments," Helena said firmly. "Consider it a test run for the cookbook recipe testing we'll be doing in January. Besides, someone needs to be here early to handle deliveries, and we all know I'm always up at dawn."

By evening, they had a plan in place. The charity dinner would happen as scheduled, the house repairs were underway, and their temporary living arrangements were sorted. The cottage, when they finally moved in that night, proved to be surprisingly cozy. Helena's renovation choices reflected a perfect blend of modern convenience and historic charm.

"She's really changing," Stephanie mused as she and Jack settled into their temporary bedroom. "The Helena I knew in New York would never have offered her space like this."

"The Helena you knew in New York didn't know what she was missing," Jack replied, helping Tessa onto her new bed – a plush doggy mattress Helena had apparently ordered specifically for her. "Speaking of missing things, look what I found while checking the house damage."

He pulled out a small, leather-bound book – another of Elizabeth's journals.

"This one's different," he said, handling it carefully. "It's her personal Christmas journal. Look at this entry."

Stephanie read aloud: "December 15, 1893. Today we hosted the first annual Christmas dinner for those in need. Some said it was improper to open my bakery for such a purpose, that it would damage its reputation as a fine establishment. But I believe that true success is measured not in dollars and cents, but in the number of lives we touch. Besides, there is something magical about seeing joy spread through the simple act of sharing food and fellowship."

"She did the same thing," Stephanie realized. "A hundred and thirty years ago, Elizabeth Fields opened her bakery to the community, just like we're doing now."

"There's more," Jack turned to a later entry. "She writes about how that dinner became one of Sweet Pine Valley's most beloved traditions. How it brought the town together year after year, through good times and bad."

"And now we're carrying on that tradition," Stephanie smiled, "in ways we didn't even know about."

A knock at their door interrupted them. Sarah poked her head in, holding her phone.

"You need to see this," she said excitedly. "Someone posted a photo of our window display on social media. It's going viral! People are calling it 'The Christmas Time Capsule' because of how it blends historical elements with modern techniques. Helena's already had calls from three magazines wanting to do features."

"That's not all," Tom added, joining them. "The story about the charity dinner moving to the bakery has caught attention too. People are calling it a 'full-circle moment' – a Fields once again opening the bakery doors to the community at Christmas."

"Speaking of opening doors," Helena's voice came from behind them. She stood in the hallway, still wearing her coat. "I've just come from the bakery. You need to see this."

They followed her outside, where the storm clouds had finally cleared, revealing a sky full of stars. The bakery's window display glowed like a beacon in the night, but it wasn't alone. All along Main Street, other businesses had turned on their Christmas lights, creating a pathway of warmth and color through the snow.

And there, making their way toward the bakery, was a group of townspeople carrying casseroles, decorations, and supplies for the charity dinner.

"We thought you might need help getting ready," Mrs. Henderson called out, leading the group. "Consider it our way of saying thank you – for carrying on Elizabeth's legacy, and for creating your own."

The next hour was filled with the kind of organized chaos that only small towns can create. Tables were set up, decorations were arranged, and Helena – to everyone's amazement – taught the high school students her secret recipe for hot chocolate.

"You know," she said later, as they all sat around one of the tables, enjoying cups of that same hot chocolate, "I came to Sweet Pine Valley thinking I had something to teach. But it turns out, I had more to learn."

"We all did," Stephanie agreed, watching as Tessa made her rounds, receiving pets and treats from their impromptu gathering. "About community, about legacy, about what really matters."

"About home," Jack added softly, squeezing her hand.

Outside, snow began to fall again – gently this time, as if the weather too had learned something about moderation. The window display cast rainbow shadows across the fresh snow, while Elizabeth's cookie cutter caught the light just so, seeming to wink at them all.

Tomorrow would bring more preparations, more renovations, more challenges and joys. But tonight, in the warm glow of the bakery, surrounded by friends and family both old and new, they were exactly where they needed to be.

After all, as Elizabeth had written in her journal: "Christmas magic isn't found in perfect moments, but in perfectly imperfect ones – in damaged roofs that lead to opened doors, in storms that bring people together, and in the simple act of sharing what we have with those who need it."

Chapter 9

Sweet Tidings

The morning of the Christmas charity dinner dawned with crystalline clarity, sunlight sparkling off snow-laden branches outside Helena's cottage where Stephanie and Jack had temporarily made their home. The aroma of fresh coffee mingled with the crisp winter air sneaking through the window frame as Stephanie stood at the vintage dresser, fastening the antique snowflake necklace Jack had surprised her with the night before – another treasure found in Elizabeth's belongings.

"It suits you," Jack's voice came warm against her ear as he wrapped his arms around her waist, the wool of his sweater soft against her back. "Though not as much as that smile you're trying to hide."

"I'm just happy," she admitted, leaning into his embrace. "Despite the roof damage, despite living in Helena's cottage, despite how crazy everything is... I'm ridiculously happy."

"Even with two hundred dinner guests arriving in—" he checked his watch, "exactly six hours?"

"Especially then." She turned in his arms, breathing in the familiar scent of his aftershave mixed with the fir-scented soap they'd found in Helena's bathroom. "It feels right, doesn't it? Carrying on Elizabeth's tradition?"

Before Jack could answer, Tessa came skittering into the room, her nails clicking on the hardwood floors. She carried her leash in her mouth – a new habit that showed just how far their timid rescue had come.

"Someone's eager for their morning walk," Jack laughed, reluctantly releasing Stephanie. "Want to join us? The bakery prep can wait another hour."

The streets of Sweet Pine Valley were already buzzing with pre-dinner activity despite the early hour. Holiday music drifted from the town speakers, mixing with the sound of shovels scraping sidewalks and children's laughter from the park where an impromptu snowman-building contest had broken out.

"Jack! Stephanie!" Sarah's voice carried across the square. She hurried toward them, her cheeks pink from the cold, clutching what looked like architectural plans. "Wait until you see what Tom found in the house's walls!"

The renovation crew, working on repairing the storm damage, had discovered a hidden compartment behind the kitchen's original cabinets. Inside were Elizabeth Fields' original house plans – including detailed drawings for a spring garden that had never been implemented.

"Look at this," Sarah spread the yellowed papers carefully on a nearby bench. "She designed a complete Victorian kitchen garden, with herbs, vegetables, even a small greenhouse. And these notes in the margin – they're recipes! Ways to use everything she planned to grow."

"That would be perfect for the cookbook," Stephanie mused, studying the elegant handwriting. "We could do a whole section on garden-to-table baking, using Elizabeth's original ideas but with modern twists."

"Speaking of twists," Jack cleared his throat, suddenly looking nervous. "There's something else you should see."

He led them around the corner to the house, where despite the renovation tarps and equipment, something magical had happened. The entire wraparound porch was decorated with twinkling lights and fresh garland. In the front window – now properly repaired and weatherproofed – stood a magnificent Christmas tree.

"Tom's crew finished the major repairs yesterday," Jack explained. "I thought... well, I thought maybe we could host Christmas here after all. It won't be fully renovated, but the important rooms are done. We could have our first holiday in our real home."

Stephanie felt tears welling up as she took in the scene. The tree's lights reflected in the antique window glass, creating a warm glow that seemed to welcome them home. Tessa pranced up the porch steps as if she already knew this was where she belonged.

"You did all this? When?"

"Had some help," he admitted. "Helena supervised the tree decorating – turns out she has quite an eye for ornament placement. And Sarah's been storing all the vintage decorations we found properly sorted and labeled."

"That's not all," Sarah added with a grin. "Show her the best part."

Jack led Stephanie up the porch steps and opened the front door. The entryway, now restored to its original glory, took her breath away. The woodwork gleamed warmly, and the stained glass window on the landing cast colored shadows across the walls. But it was the smell that brought tears to her eyes – the distinctive scent of Christmas cookies baking.

"Helena's been busy this morning," Jack explained softly. "She said every new home needs to be broken in with the smell of baking. Something about creating memories before we even move in."

In the kitchen – now a perfect blend of Victorian charm and modern functionality – they found Helena surrounded by cooling racks of cookies. She wore one of Elizabeth's vintage aprons, discovered in the attic and carefully restored.

"Don't get too excited," she said without looking up from her piping. "These are for the charity dinner. But I thought... well, I thought the house needed to remember what it was meant for. A home where love and baking come together."

Stephanie moved to help with the cookies, falling into an easy rhythm with her former mentor. Jack and Sarah went to check on the final renovation details, while Tessa settled into a patch of sunlight streaming through the new kitchen windows.

"I've been thinking," Helena said after a while, her focus still on the intricate icing design she was creating. "About Elizabeth's garden plans. The cottage has enough space... if you wouldn't mind sharing the bounty with a neighbor?"

"You want to plant the garden?"

"Why not? It would be perfect for the cookbook project. And..." Helena hesitated, something Stephanie had rarely seen her do, "I find I rather like the idea of putting down roots. Literally and figuratively."

Before Stephanie could respond, Jack returned with news from Tom. The last of the repairs were complete – they could move back in whenever they were ready. "Though," he added with a twinkle in his eye, "Helena's welcome to keep baking Christmas cookies here anytime."

The rest of the morning passed in a whirl of preparation for the charity dinner. The bakery had been transformed into a winter wonderland, with Elizabeth's vintage decorations adding authentic charm to every table. The window display continued to draw admirers, its sugar sculptures casting rainbow patterns across the fresh snow outside.

By late afternoon, the first guests began arriving. Families with children, elderly couples, college students who couldn't make it home for the holidays – all were welcomed with warm smiles and hot chocolate. Helena, to everyone's surprise, proved to be excellent with the children, teaching impromptu cookie-decorating lessons at a special table.

"Look at this," Jack whispered to Stephanie, nodding toward where Helena was showing a small girl how to pipe the perfect snowflake. "Who would have thought the famous Chef Drake had such a soft spot for kids?"

"She's full of surprises lately," Stephanie agreed, leaning into him. "Like someone else I know who secretly decorated our house for Christmas."

"Speaking of surprises," he turned her gently to face the bakery window. Outside, fat snowflakes had begun to fall, dancing in the glow of the Christmas lights. "Care to take a walk? Just for a minute?"

They slipped out into the gentle snowfall, leaving Sarah and Helena to manage the dinner. Jack led her to the town square, where the giant Christmas tree sparkled with thousands of lights.

"I have something for you," he said, reaching into his pocket. "Another piece of Elizabeth's legacy, but this one... this one means something special."

He held out a small, velvet box. Inside was a delicate gold ring set with tiny pearls in a snowflake pattern.

"It was Elizabeth's engagement ring," he explained softly. "Her husband had it made specially for her by a local jeweler. I found it with her journals, along with a note saying it should go to 'the next Fields baker who finds her true love.' I know you already have an engagement ring, but I thought... maybe this could be your wedding band?"

Stephanie felt tears freezing on her cheeks as she nodded, too moved to speak. Jack slipped the ring onto her right hand for safekeeping, the antique gold warm against her skin.

"It's perfect," she finally managed. "Like everything else about this crazy, wonderful life we're building."

The sound of carolers drifted from the bakery, where the charity dinner was in full swing. Through the window, they could see Helena demonstrating proper whipped cream technique to an attentive audience. Sarah was arranging more of Elizabeth's decorations while Tom added wood to the old stove they'd restored. Tessa supervised it all from her special cushion near the display window, occasionally accepting gentle pets from passing children.

"Should we go back in?" Jack asked, brushing snow from Stephanie's hair.

"In a minute," she said, pulling him close for a kiss that tasted of snowflakes and possibility. "I just want to remember this moment. Our first Christmas in Sweet Pine Valley as almost-husband-and-wife, surrounded by all this love and history and magic."

Above them, the snow continued to fall, each flake catching the Christmas lights like tiny stars falling to earth. From the bakery came the sounds of laughter and joy, the very things Elizabeth had wished for when she hosted her first charity dinner so many years ago.

And in that moment, standing in the swirling snow with the man she loved, Stephanie knew that some traditions were meant to be carried forward, some legacies were meant to be found, and some loves were simply meant to be.

Chapter 10

Christmas Memories in the Making

The week before Christmas transformed Sweet Pine Valley into a snow globe scene come to life. Fresh powder dusted the Victorian house's newly repaired roof, while garlands and twinkling lights adorned every porch column. Inside, the blend of renovation dust and Christmas magic created an atmosphere that was uniquely theirs.

"Careful with those!" Helena called as Tom and Jack maneuvered an antique china cabinet through the front door. "That's been in my family for three generations."

Stephanie paused in her cookie dough mixing to watch through the kitchen's new bay window as Helena supervised the moving of her personal belongings into the cottage. The renowned chef had officially given up her New York apartment, committing fully to small-town life.

"Never thought I'd see Helena Drake directing traffic in snow boots," Sarah mused, joining Stephanie at the window. She was armed with fabric swatches for the wedding planning they were supposed to be doing. "Though I never thought I'd see her in an ugly Christmas sweater either, and yet..."

They both glanced toward the cottage where Helena was indeed wearing a bright red sweater adorned with sparkly candy canes – a gift from the Sweet Pine Valley Knitting Club, who had adopted her as their newest member.

"Everything's changing," Stephanie said softly, rolling out another batch of her great-grandmother's sugar cookies. "In the best possible way."

"Speaking of changes," Sarah spread the fabric swatches across the new kitchen island, "we need to make some decisions about the wedding. December might seem far away, but—"

She was interrupted by a commotion from the front yard. Tessa's excited barking mixed with exclamations of surprise. They rushed to the window to find Jack and Tom staring at something inside the china cabinet they'd been moving.

"Stephanie!" Jack called, his voice carrying an odd note of excitement. "You need to see this!"

The cabinet, temporarily resting in the front yard, had a false back that had come loose during the move. Behind it was a collection of old letters, photographs, and what appeared to be a diary.

"Those aren't mine," Helena frowned, examining the weathered papers. "This cabinet came from my grandmother's estate sale in Vermont thirty years ago..."

"Look at this," Jack carefully extracted a photograph. It showed a group of people standing in front of a familiar Victorian house – their house. And there, in the center, was Elizabeth Fields alongside a woman who could have been Helena's twin.

"That's my grandmother," Helena whispered, taking the photograph with trembling hands. "But how..."

Stephanie was already reading one of the letters. "Dear Elizabeth, Thank you for taking me under your wing this summer. Your teaching has transformed not just my baking but my understanding of what it means to create a true home..."

"My grandmother apprenticed here?" Helena sat down heavily on the cabinet's packaging. "She learned to bake from Elizabeth Fields?"

"Not just that," Stephanie continued reading. "According to these letters, she lived in the cottage while she trained. Elizabeth was teaching her both baking and business management. She writes about wanting to open her own bakery someday..."

"Which she did," Helena finished. "In Burlington. The bakery I grew up in, where I learned to love cooking..." She looked around at the house, the cottage, the town square visible in the distance. "I thought coming here was a random choice, but..."

"Nothing about Sweet Pine Valley is random," Mrs. Henderson's voice made them all turn. She stood at the garden gate, holding what appeared to be yet another box of old papers. "When I saw Helena's name on the cottage purchase papers, I started doing some research. Your grandmother, Sophie Drake, was one of Elizabeth's most successful students."

The next hour was spent in the warmth of their kitchen, spreading the newly discovered documents across the island while Helena's belongings sat forgotten in the snow. The story that emerged was remarkable: Sophie Drake had come to Sweet Pine Valley in 1925, a young woman with dreams of becoming a baker. Elizabeth Fields, then in her later years, had taken her in, teaching her everything she knew.

"The Drake family bakery in Burlington," Mrs. Henderson explained, "was started with Elizabeth's blessing – and her recipes. She believed in expanding the reach of good food and community, not restricting it. Sophie's success wasn't competition; it was continuation."

"That's why the cottage felt like home," Helena mused, running her fingers over her grandmother's handwriting. "Why this whole town felt familiar somehow..." She looked at Stephanie with new understanding. "And why I was drawn to teach you in New York, though you reminded me of no one I could name at the time."

"The Fields-Drake connection comes full circle," Sarah said softly. "Just in time for Christmas."

"And the wedding," Jack added, wrapping an arm around Stephanie. "Speaking of which..."

He nodded toward one particular letter they hadn't opened yet. The envelope was marked "For the next Fields baker's wedding day" in Elizabeth's distinctive handwriting.

Stephanie opened it carefully, the paper fragile with age. Inside was a recipe – but not just any recipe. It was Elizabeth's secret wedding cake recipe, the one that had made Fields of Sweet Dreams famous in the late 1800s.

"It's all here," Stephanie breathed. "The special techniques, the unique ingredients... She notes that she only made it for the most special occasions, for couples whose love stories were meant to be part of Sweet Pine Valley's history."

"Well then," Helena straightened, suddenly every inch the master chef despite her Christmas sweater, "we better start testing it. A recipe this special needs to be perfect for next December."

The rest of the day took on a magical quality. While Tom and Jack finally finished moving Helena's furniture, the three women worked in the kitchen, bringing Elizabeth's recipe to life. Tessa supervised from her new window seat, occasionally reminding them that quality control should include sharing with puppies.

"The texture is remarkable," Helena noted as they sampled their first attempt. "The way she incorporated local maple syrup with traditional European techniques... It's revolutionary even by today's standards."

"Like Elizabeth herself," Mrs. Henderson added. She'd stayed to help, sharing more town history as they baked. "She was always pushing boundaries, finding ways to blend tradition with innovation."

"Rather like someone else I know," Jack said, stealing a taste of frosting and earning a playful swat from Stephanie. "A certain baker who combined New York training with small-town heart..."

As evening fell, the kitchen filled with the warm glow of Christmas lights reflecting off new snow. Helena's china cabinet, now properly placed in the cottage, stood ready to hold new memories. The test cakes cooled on vintage racks while Christmas cookies baked, filling both houses with the scent of sweet possibilities.

"I've been thinking," Helena said as they all gathered for an impromptu dinner of soup and fresh bread. "About the cookbook. What if we expanded it? Not just current recipes, but the whole history – Elizabeth's influence, my grandmother's journey, the way these traditions have shaped multiple generations of bakers..."

"A love letter to small-town baking," Stephanie nodded. "And to Sweet Pine Valley itself."

"Speaking of love letters," Sarah pulled out her wedding planning notebook. "Now that we have the cake sorted, we should talk about the ceremony. I've been sketching some ideas..."

Her designs captured everything they'd discussed – the vintage elements, the personal touches, the blend of past and present that seemed to define their life in Sweet Pine Valley. But she'd added something new: a garden archway, designed using Elizabeth's recently discovered plans.

"I thought," she explained, "if Helena's going to plant the kitchen garden in spring, by next December it would be perfect. You could get married under an arch of climbing roses, right where Elizabeth planned her own garden entrance."

"Using flowers grown in soil that's seen generations of love stories," Jack mused. "I like it."

Later that night, after everyone had gone home and the houses had settled into peaceful silence, Stephanie and Jack stood on their porch, watching snow fall in the Christmas lights' glow. Tessa dozed in Jack's arms, worn out from all the day's excitement.

"You know what I love most about today's discovery?" Jack asked softly.

"What's that?"

"It proves what I've always suspected – that some loves are meant to be, some places call to our hearts, and some stories are written long before we know we're part of them."

From the cottage came the sound of Helena's classical music – a new addition to Sweet Pine Valley's nighttime symphony. The Christmas lights twinkled against fresh snow, and somewhere in the distance, church bells chimed.

"Next Christmas," Stephanie said, touching Elizabeth's ring where it still sat on her right hand, waiting for their wedding day, "we'll be married. Standing right here, making new memories in this house that's seen so much love."

"With a garden full of Elizabeth's flowers, a kitchen full of shared recipes, and hearts full of small-town magic," Jack agreed. "Though I have to admit, I never expected Helena Drake to be such a big part of our story."

"I think Elizabeth did," Stephanie smiled. "She seems to have planned quite a bit of this, in her way. The house, the recipes, the garden... even Helena finding her way back to her grandmother's path."

"Think she planned for a dachshund in a Christmas sweater too?" Jack laughed as Tessa snuffled in her sleep, her own holiday-themed sweater (another gift from the knitting club) slightly askew.

"Probably not," Stephanie conceded. "But I like to think she'd approve. After all, homes are built on love in all its forms – even the four-legged kind."

They stayed on the porch a while longer, watching the snow fall, listening to the peaceful sounds of their two houses settling into night. Tomorrow would bring more wedding planning, more cookbook development, more preparations for their first Christmas in their true home.

But for now, wrapped in the warmth of love and history, they simply existed in this perfect moment – a moment that had been written in the stars, hidden in china cabinets, and tucked into the heart of Sweet Pine Valley all along.

"Merry Christmas, almost-wife," Jack whispered.

"Merry Christmas, almost-husband," Stephanie replied.

And somewhere, perhaps, Elizabeth Fields and Sophie Drake smiled down on the legacy they'd helped create – a legacy of love, baking, and the simple magic of finding exactly where you're meant to be.

Chapter 11

Hearts and Hearths

Christmas Eve arrived with unexpected news. Stephanie woke to find Jack already dressed and pacing their bedroom, phone in hand, his expression a mix of excitement and concern.

"That was Dr. Thompson," he said when he noticed she was awake. "He's been offered a position at a veterinary teaching hospital in Colorado. They want him to start in February."

"But he was supposed to stay on part-time through next summer," Stephanie sat up, immediately understanding the implications. "To help with the transition..."

"Exactly." Jack ran a hand through his hair, a gesture she recognized as his thinking mode. "He wants to take the position – it's a dream opportunity for him. But it means I'll be running the practice entirely on my own, months earlier than planned."

Tessa, sensing the tension, hopped onto the bed and nestled between them, offering her own form of comfort.

"You can do this," Stephanie said firmly, reaching for his hand. "You're more than ready."

"That's not all," Jack sat on the bed's edge. "The teaching hospital... they want me too. They've offered me a position as well. Full professorship, state-of-the-art facilities, salary that would make the house renovation look like pocket change..."

The words hung in the air like frost, delicate and potentially devastating. Outside, snow began to fall, adding to the hushed tension of the moment.

"When do they need an answer?" Stephanie's voice was barely a whisper.

"January 15th." He squeezed her hand. "But Stephanie, I wouldn't even consider it without—"

A knock at their door interrupted them. Helena stood there, still in her robe but clutching a manila envelope.

"Sorry to interrupt," she said, taking in their serious expressions, "but this was just delivered by private courier. It's from Le Cordon Bleu Paris."

Now it was Stephanie's turn to feel the world tilt on its axis. She'd applied to their prestigious visiting chef program years ago, before leaving New York, before Sweet Pine Valley, before Jack. She'd almost forgotten about it.

"They want me for their spring guest chef series," she breathed, scanning the letter. "Three months in Paris, teaching advanced pastry techniques, plus..." she swallowed hard, "they're interested in publishing our cookbook as part of their culinary heritage series. They want both Helena and me to expand it into a full teaching curriculum."

"Paris?" Jack's voice cracked slightly.

"Paris," Helena confirmed. "It's an incredible opportunity, Stephanie. The kind that changes careers. Changes lives."

Before anyone could say more, Sarah burst in through the front door downstairs, her voice carrying up the stairs. "Emergency wedding crisis! The venue we wanted for the reception just booked another event for next December! We need to either change our date or—"

She stopped short at seeing their faces as she reached the bedroom door. "What's wrong? What did I miss?"

The next hour was spent in the kitchen, where Helena stress-baked Christmas cookies while they shared their respective news. Tom joined them, having been called by Sarah, and soon the room was filled with the scent of gingerbread and the weight of decisions.

"You can't pass up Colorado," Sarah told Jack. "It's a teaching position at one of the best veterinary hospitals in the country."

"And Paris?" Tom added, looking at Stephanie. "That's the opportunity of a lifetime."

"But what about the house?" Stephanie gestured around them. "The bakery? The cookbook as it is now? Our wedding..."

"The house will wait," Helena said quietly. She'd been uncharacteristically silent until now. "Houses always do. But opportunities like these... they're rare. Like finding your grandmother's letters in my china cabinet – some things are meant to be, even if their timing seems impossible."

"We could postpone the wedding," Sarah suggested carefully. "Take time to explore these opportunities, then come back and—"

"No." Jack and Stephanie spoke simultaneously.

"I mean," Stephanie continued, "these are amazing opportunities, but..."

"But this is home," Jack finished. "This house, this town, these people – this is where we're meant to be."

Helena set down her piping bag with unusual force. "Is it? Or is that just the safe choice? Stephanie, when you came to my class in New York, you were hungry for knowledge, for growth, for challenges. And Jack, you've talked about wanting to teach, to share your skills with the next generation of veterinarians. Are you both really willing to give up those dreams?"

"Sometimes," came Mrs. Henderson's voice from the doorway, making them all jump, "the biggest dreams are the smallest ones."

She joined them at the kitchen island, adding her own tin of Christmas cookies to Helena's growing collection. "Elizabeth Fields was offered a position at a prestigious hotel in New York once. And Sophie Drake had a chance to study in France. They both chose to stay in Vermont instead."

"Because they were afraid of change?" Helena challenged.

"No," Mrs. Henderson smiled. "Because they recognized that their real dreams weren't about places or positions. They were about creating something lasting, something that mattered. Elizabeth's letter about it is quite beautiful – it's in that collection you found, Helena, though you might not have gotten to it yet."

Stephanie and Jack exchanged glances. They hadn't read all the letters yet, saving them for quiet moments together.

"What did she say?" Stephanie asked softly.

Mrs. Henderson closed her eyes, reciting from memory: "The world offers many glittering paths, but the truest path is the one that leads you home. Not to a place, but to your heart's deepest purpose. New York would make me famous, but Sweet Pine Valley makes me whole."

The kitchen fell silent except for the timer dinging on Helena's latest batch of cookies. Outside, the snow continued to fall, and somewhere in the distance, church bells began to ring – Sweet Pine Valley's traditional Christmas Eve carol.

"I have an idea," Helena said suddenly. "One that might solve everything." She looked at Stephanie. "What if we brought Paris here?"

"What do you mean?"

"The cookbook – it's already unique. A blend of traditional small-town baking with modern techniques. What if we proposed a different kind of partnership with Le Cordon Bleu? Instead of you going to Paris, we invite their students here. Create a special summer program focusing on American heritage baking, small-town traditions with a modern twist."

"Using Elizabeth's recipes," Stephanie caught on, excitement building. "And Sophie's innovations..."

"And your creative adaptations," Helena nodded. "We could hold classes in both the bakery and my cottage kitchen. Create a true farm-to-table experience using the garden we're planning..."

"The garden!" Sarah exclaimed. "That's it! Jack, what if you did the same thing with the veterinary program? Instead of teaching in Colorado, what if you created a rural veterinary experience program here? Partner with the teaching hospital but keep your practice. Students could come learn about small-town veterinary care, the unique challenges and rewards..."

"Using Dr. Thompson's connections," Tom added. "He could help set it up before he leaves, introduce you to the right people..."

"And the wedding," Sarah continued, now in full planning mode, "we could still have it next December, but make it part of the whole picture. A celebration not just of your marriage, but of everything you're building here. The programs, the partnerships, the way you're expanding Sweet Pine Valley's legacy while staying true to its heart..."

Jack and Stephanie looked at each other across the kitchen island. The same understanding passed between them – this was right. This was their path.

"It would be a lot of work," Jack said slowly. "Setting up both programs, running them while maintaining our regular businesses..."

"Good thing you have help," Helena said firmly. "I didn't give up my New York life to sit around baking cookies – though these are excellent, if I do say so myself." She handed around a plate of perfectly decorated gingerbread stars.

"And you have us," Sarah added, Tom nodding beside her.

"And the whole town," Mrs. Henderson smiled. "You'd be amazed how many people here have skills to share, stories to tell, wisdom to pass on."

"Like Elizabeth and Sophie," Stephanie mused. "They didn't just teach baking – they taught a way of life. A way of building community through sharing what you love."

"Exactly," Jack pulled her close. "And isn't that worth more than any position in Colorado?"

"Or Paris?" she smiled up at him.

"Paris," Helena sniffed, "is overrated in December anyway."

The rest of Christmas Eve unfolded like a gift itself. They called Dr. Thompson, who was thrilled with the idea of helping establish a rural veterinary program. Helena drafted a preliminary proposal for Le Cordon Bleu, her enthusiasm for the project showing in every carefully worded paragraph.

Sarah and Tom strung the last of the Christmas lights, making both the house and cottage glow like beacons in the falling snow. Mrs. Henderson brought more town records, showing how Elizabeth and Sophie had collaborated on their own teaching programs years ago.

As evening settled over Sweet Pine Valley, they gathered in the living room around the Christmas tree. Tessa wore her new holiday bow (the knitting club had outdone themselves), and Helena had traded her usual elegant attire for one of Stephanie's comfortable sweaters.

"To choices," Jack raised his hot chocolate, made from Helena's secret recipe.

"To changes," Stephanie added.

"To staying true to your heart," Helena surprised them all by adding, "even when it leads you somewhere you never expected."

"To Sweet Pine Valley," Mrs. Henderson smiled, "where dreams don't have to be big to be important."

"And to Elizabeth and Sophie," Sarah concluded, "who knew all along that the best legacy is one that grows and changes while keeping its roots strong."

Outside, carolers began their traditional Christmas Eve journey through town. The snow created halos around the Christmas lights, and through the window, they could see families heading toward the town square for the annual Christmas Eve gathering.

"Ready to join them?" Jack asked softly.

Stephanie looked around at their collected family – blood and chosen – at their home filled with history and hope, at the plans already taking shape for their future.

"Ready," she said. "For everything."

They walked to the town square together, their footsteps adding to the countless others that had traveled this path before them. The town Christmas tree sparkled, and as they joined the gathering crowd, Stephanie felt the rightness of their decision settle into her bones like warming honey.

Sometimes, she realized, the biggest dreams come wrapped in small-town packages. And sometimes, the truest paths are the ones that lead you right back home.

Chapter 12

Sweet Dreams and New Beginnings

The week between Christmas and New Year's brought both unexpected warmth and surprising developments to Sweet Pine Valley. The unusual January thaw revealed the bare bones of Helena's future garden, while the last of the house renovations neared completion.

"Look what the snow was hiding," Helena called from the cottage yard one unusually mild morning. She stood over what appeared to be an old stone pathway, partially uncovered by the melting snow. "It matches Elizabeth's garden plans exactly!"

Stephanie joined her, Tessa prancing ahead to investigate this new discovery. The path's worn stones told stories of countless footsteps, of gatherings and teachings long past.

"There's more," Tom said, emerging from the house with another set of blueprints. "We found these behind the new kitchen cabinets during the final installation. They're Sophie's additions to Elizabeth's original garden design – notes about which plants thrived, which struggled, even suggestions for future improvements."

"It's like they're still teaching us," Stephanie mused, examining the detailed notes. "Still showing us the way forward."

"Speaking of moving forward," Jack appeared from the direction of Dr. Thompson's clinic, his expression bright with excitement. "I just got off a video call with the veterinary teaching hospital. They love our rural practice program idea. In fact..." he paused for dramatic effect, "they want to make it a formal part of their curriculum. Two months here would be required for all senior students specializing in rural veterinary medicine."

"Jack, that's wonderful!" Stephanie hugged him tightly. "When would it start?"

"That's the best part – they want to launch this spring. Dr. Thompson can help set everything up before he leaves for Colorado. And..." he grinned, "they're offering grant funding to expand the clinic. We can add the teaching facilities we'll need without touching our house renovation budget."

Helena, who had been unusually quiet, suddenly spoke up. "I just received similar news from Le Cordon Bleu." She held up her phone. "They're not only interested in our heritage baking program – they want to feature Sweet Pine Valley in their upcoming documentary series about traditional American baking. They'll be here next week to film a pilot episode."

"Next week?" Stephanie felt her knees go weak. "But we haven't even finished organizing Elizabeth's recipes, or tested all the techniques, or—"

"Or remembered to breathe?" Sarah appeared at the garden gate, laden with wedding planning books. "Don't panic. This is perfect timing actually. Show them the real Sweet Pine Valley – a place where old and new, traditional and modern, all come together naturally."

"Like Elizabeth's garden design meeting Sophie's practical experience," Tom added, gesturing to the uncovered path.

"Exactly," Helena nodded. "They don't want polished perfection. They want authenticity – the story of how a small town keeps its baking heritage alive while embracing change."

The next few days passed in a whirl of activity. The bakery hummed with energy as they tested Elizabeth's recipes, each one revealing new secrets. Helena's usually pristine kitchen became a happy chaos of flour and friendship as Sarah helped document each step for both the documentary and their expanded cookbook.

Jack's clinic underwent its own transformation. The old storage room, once filled with outdated equipment, became a bright classroom space. Dr. Thompson spent hours sharing his decades of experience, which Tom carefully recorded for future students.

"It's not just about medicine," Dr. Thompson explained as they organized his old case files. "It's about understanding the rhythm of a small town, the way each animal is part of a family's story."

One evening, as they all gathered in the newly finished kitchen for dinner, Mrs. Henderson brought over a surprising discovery – a collection of old photographs showing Elizabeth teaching in her garden.

"These were in the historical society archives," she explained, spreading them across the kitchen island. "Look at how she arranged her outdoor classroom."

The photos showed students gathered around garden beds, learning about herbs and their uses in baking. Elizabeth stood among them, pointing out different plants, while Sophie could be seen taking careful notes.

"We could do the same," Helena mused, studying the images. "Use the garden as both a teaching space and a source of ingredients. The Le Cordon Bleu students could learn about growing what they bake..."

"And the veterinary students could help maintain it," Jack added. "Understanding local flora is crucial for treating farm animals."

"Plus," Sarah chimed in, "it would make a perfect setting for the wedding. Imagine exchanging vows surrounded by the same herbs and flowers Elizabeth used to teach with..."

Stephanie felt tears welling up as she looked at the old photographs. "They really did think of everything, didn't they? Elizabeth and Sophie – they created something so much bigger than themselves."

"And now we get to carry it forward," Jack wrapped an arm around her. "In our own way."

The week culminated in an unexpected gathering. As news of the Le Cordon Bleu documentary spread, townspeople began bringing their own family recipes and stories to share. The bakery's front room became an impromptu museum of Sweet Pine Valley's culinary history.

"My grandmother learned to make these rolls from Elizabeth herself," Mrs. Thompson from the bookshop explained, demonstrating the unique folding technique. "She said Elizabeth believed every recipe carried a piece of home."

"And these cookie cutters," Mr. Henderson added, carefully unwrapping a set that looked remarkably like Elizabeth's, "were made by the same craftsman who made hers. Sophie ordered an extra set for my mother when she was starting her own bakery."

As they recorded these stories and techniques for the documentary, Stephanie realized they were capturing something far more precious than just recipes. They were preserving a legacy of community, of sharing knowledge and nurturing dreams.

The morning the Le Cordon Bleu film crew arrived brought crisp, clear weather. The garden path, now fully uncovered, led them from the bakery to the cottage, where Helena had prepared a display of both traditional and innovative pastries.

"This is extraordinary," the director commented, filming as Helena demonstrated Elizabeth's unique way of laminating dough. "The way you've maintained these historical techniques while adapting them for modern kitchens..."

"That's the heart of Sweet Pine Valley," Stephanie explained, working alongside her former mentor. "We don't just preserve the past – we help it grow into the future."

The documentary filming flowed naturally into a town-wide baking demonstration. Residents shared their stories on camera, each one adding a new layer to Sweet Pine Valley's rich tapestry. Even Tessa got her moment of fame, charming the crew with her careful supervision of quality control.

"This is more than we hoped for," the producer told them later. "We came expecting to film a cooking show, but we've found a story about legacy, about community, about dreams that span generations."

As evening fell, they gathered in the garden. The unusual warmth had held, allowing them to set up tables outside. Helena's students from New York, who had arrived to help with the filming, mingled with local bakers. Dr. Thompson's colleagues from the teaching hospital chatted with townspeople about the rural veterinary program.

"Look at this," Jack murmured to Stephanie as they stood on the porch, watching their various worlds blend together. "Elizabeth's garden is already bringing people together, even before we've planted anything."

"Speaking of planting," Helena joined them, holding what appeared to be yet another old document. "I found this in Sophie's notes. It's a planting calendar, coordinated with the phases of the moon. She believed timing was crucial for both gardens and dreams."

"According to this," Sarah peered at the calendar, "we should start the herb garden on the next new moon – which happens to be..."

"The day the first veterinary students arrive," Jack finished. "Perfect timing."

"And look at this note," Tom pointed to Sophie's elegant handwriting in the margin. "She writes that Elizabeth always said new ventures should begin with community support. That's why they held their first classes during the town's spring festival."

Mrs. Henderson, overhearing, smiled knowingly. "Which is exactly when your programs will be starting. Some patterns are meant to repeat."

As night fell, someone started playing music – old folk tunes that had probably been heard in this same garden decades ago. The film crew, long since finished with official documenting, joined in the impromptu celebration.

"To new beginnings," Helena raised her glass, looking more relaxed than Stephanie had ever seen her. "And to old wisdom showing us the way."

"To Sweet Pine Valley," Jack added, "where dreams take root and grow."

"To Elizabeth and Sophie," Sarah and Tom chimed in, "who knew that the best lessons are taught with love."

"And to us," Stephanie whispered to Jack as they swayed to the music. "For finding our way home."

Later that night, after the guests had gone and the garden lay quiet under the stars, Stephanie stood at the kitchen window. She could see the path gleaming in the moonlight, leading from the house to the cottage, from the past to the future.

Jack joined her, wrapping his arms around her from behind. "Penny for your thoughts?"

"I was just thinking about choices," she said softly. "About how sometimes the biggest dreams come true in the smallest ways."

"Like finding your great-great-grandmother's recipes?"

"Like finding everything we never knew we were looking for," she corrected. "A home, a purpose, a way to honor the past while building something new..."

"A family," he added, as Tessa padded over to lean against their legs. From the cottage, they could hear Helena humming as she prepared for the next day's filming.

"A family," Stephanie agreed. "In all its wonderful, unexpected forms."

Tomorrow would bring more filming, more planning, more steps toward their expanding dreams. But tonight, in their nearly-finished home, surrounded by the echoes of those who had dreamed here before them, everything was perfectly, wonderfully right.

After all, as Elizabeth had written in one of her recently discovered letters: "The sweetest dreams are those we dare to make real, one day and one heart at a time."

Chapter 13

Spring Blossoms and Growing Pains

Spring arrived in Sweet Pine Valley with both promise and challenges. The garden's first tender shoots pushed through the warming soil, mirroring the growth of Jack and Stephanie's new ventures. But with growth came unexpected complications.

"They want to what?" Stephanie stared at Helena across the cottage's kitchen counter, where they'd been reviewing the Le Cordon Bleu contract.

"Expand the program," Helena repeated, her usually steady voice carrying a note of concern. "They're not just interested in the heritage baking course anymore. They want to establish a full culinary arts satellite campus here in Sweet Pine Valley."

"But that would mean..."

"More students, more facilities, more changes." Helena gestured to the preliminary plans the school had sent. "They're proposing to buy the old mill building downtown, renovate it into teaching kitchens and classrooms. They want year-round programs, not just summer sessions."

Before Stephanie could process this, Jack burst in, his own expression a mix of excitement and worry. "The veterinary teaching hospital just called. They're doubling the student placement numbers for fall. And..." he ran a hand through his hair, "they want to feature Sweet Pine Valley in a nationwide rural veterinary recruitment campaign."

Tessa, sensing the tension, moved between them all, offering her unique form of comfort through gentle nudges and concerned looks.

"This is what we wanted, isn't it?" Stephanie asked softly. "For our programs to succeed?"

"Yes, but—" Jack was interrupted by Sarah's arrival, her arms full of wedding planning materials and her face flushed with news.

"The historic preservation society just contacted me," she announced. "They want to designate both houses and the garden as historical landmarks. They're calling it 'The Fields-Drake Legacy Site.'"

"Which means any changes would need approval," Tom added, following his wife with more blueprints. "Including the renovations we haven't finished yet."

The kitchen fell silent except for the gentle spring breeze rustling through the newly planted herbs. Through the window, they could see the garden coming to life – Elizabeth's vision meeting Sophie's practical additions, all blending with their own modern touches.

"Maybe it's too much," Stephanie whispered. "Maybe we're trying to hold onto too many pieces of the past while building something new..."

"Or maybe," Mrs. Henderson's voice came from the doorway, making them all jump, "you're exactly where you need to be."

She joined them at the counter, placing an old leather-bound book among their scattered papers. "I found this in the town archives this morning. It's Elizabeth's personal diary from the year she almost gave up."

"Gave up?" Helena leaned forward. "Elizabeth Fields?"

Mrs. Henderson nodded. "1894 was a challenging year. The town was growing, changes were coming faster than anyone expected. Elizabeth had opportunities to expand, to modernize, to completely transform what she'd built. She wrote about feeling pulled in too many directions, afraid of losing the heart of what she'd created."

"What did she do?" Stephanie asked, though something in her heart already knew.

"She planted a garden," Mrs. Henderson smiled. "Right where you're standing now. She wrote that when everything seemed too big, too overwhelming, she needed to remember that all growth starts small. With seeds, with hope, with faith in what you're building."

"And Sophie?" Helena's voice held an unusual tremor. "What did my grandmother do when faced with similar choices?"

"She baked bread," came a new voice. They turned to find an elderly woman standing in the cottage doorway, her white hair elegantly styled and her posture straight despite her advanced years. "Every major decision, every big change, started with her basic sourdough recipe. She said it helped her remember that the simplest things are often the most important."

"Aunt Margaret?" Helena gasped. "But you're supposed to be in Florida!"

Margaret Drake, Sophie's youngest daughter and Helena's favorite aunt, smiled as she entered the kitchen. "When I heard about what you were all building here, I knew I had to come. Mother would be so proud, Helena. Not just of the teaching program, but of you finding your way back to her beginnings."

The next hour was filled with stories as Margaret shared memories of both Sophie and Elizabeth. She spoke of summer evenings in the garden, of lessons that went beyond baking to touch on life itself, of how two remarkable women had built something that could evolve without losing its heart.

"The problem isn't the growth," Margaret said finally, looking around at their worried faces. "It's forgetting why you started. Mother and Elizabeth didn't resist change – they embraced it, but always on their own terms, always keeping the community at the center."

"Like the charity dinner at Christmas," Stephanie realized. "We didn't just continue the tradition – we made it our own."

"Exactly," Mrs. Henderson nodded. "And that's what you need to do now. Don't just accept these changes – shape them to fit Sweet Pine Valley's needs."

Ideas began flowing. Jack suggested incorporating community service requirements into the veterinary program, ensuring students would understand small-town relationships, not just rural medicine.

Helena proposed making the culinary program a true farm-to-table experience, partnering with local farmers and artisans rather than building institutional facilities.

"The old mill building could become a community teaching space," Sarah suggested. "Not just for culinary students, but for anyone wanting to learn. Like Elizabeth's original classes, but on a larger scale."

"And the garden," Tom added, studying Elizabeth's original plans, "it was never meant to be just ornamental. Every plant had a purpose, a lesson to teach. We could expand that vision."

As they talked, Margaret moved around the kitchen with familiar ease, pulling out ingredients. "I think," she said, measuring flour with practiced hands, "it's time to make Sophie's bread. Some decisions need to be kneaded out."

They spent the afternoon baking together, the simple rhythm of hands in dough bringing clarity to their thoughts. Margaret shared more stories, filling in gaps in their knowledge of both Elizabeth and Sophie's legacies.

"Did you know," she said as she demonstrated Sophie's unique folding technique, "that when the Depression hit, they turned the garden into a community victory garden? Every family in Sweet Pine Valley had a plot. Elizabeth and Mother taught them not just how to grow food, but how to preserve it, use it wisely, share with neighbors."

"That's it," Stephanie said suddenly. "That's what we need to do now. Not just preserve their legacy, but grow it – make it work for today's needs while keeping their principles alive."

The solutions began taking shape, as warm and promising as the bread rising on the counter. They would accept the expanded programs but with conditions that honored Sweet Pine Valley's character. The mill would become a community education center, not just a culinary school. The veterinary program would maintain its intimate, hands-on nature despite larger numbers.

"And the historical designation?" Sarah asked.

"We accept it," Jack said firmly. "But we make sure it protects the spirit of these places, not just their structures. Elizabeth and Sophie weren't museum pieces – they were innovators, teachers, community builders."

As evening approached, the kitchen filled with the smell of fresh bread and new possibilities. Through the window, they could see the garden where spring flowers were beginning to bloom – Elizabeth's favorites, according to Margaret, now mixing with their own choices.

"There's one more thing," Margaret said, pulling a small package from her bag. "Mother left this for whoever found their way back to Sweet Pine Valley. I think she always knew someone would."

Inside was a delicate silver pendant shaped like a key, engraved with the words "Growth keeps faith with roots."

"It was Elizabeth's originally," Margaret explained. "She gave it to Mother when she first started teaching her. Now it belongs to both of you," she looked between Helena and Stephanie. "A reminder that the sweetest legacy is one that grows."

Later that night, after Margaret had been settled into Helena's guest room and the bread had been shared with neighbors, Stephanie and Jack stood in their garden. The spring air was soft with promise, carrying the scent of blooming things and fresh possibilities.

"You know what I realized today?" Jack said, pulling her close. "We're not just planning programs or preserving history. We're writing our own chapter in Sweet Pine Valley's story."

"A chapter about growth and faith," Stephanie agreed. "About finding ways to move forward without losing sight of what matters."

"Speaking of moving forward," he grinned suddenly, "Sarah mentioned the wedding dress she found in the attic might need some alterations..."

"Jack Carter, are you trying to get wedding details out of me?"

"Maybe." He kissed her softly. "Or maybe I'm just looking forward to adding our own traditions to all this history."

From the cottage came the sound of Helena and Margaret laughing over old photos, while Tessa supervised from her favorite spot near the herb garden. The bread they'd baked sat cooling in both kitchens, filling both homes with the scent of continuity and change.

Tomorrow would bring more planning, more decisions, more steps toward their expanding future. But tonight, in the garden where so many dreams had taken root, they stood together, feeling the rightness of their path.

After all, as Elizabeth had written in her diary: "The truest growth honors what came before while reaching boldly toward what might be. In this way, we keep faith with both our roots and our dreams."

Chapter 14

Summer's Promise

One week before their first students were due to arrive, Sweet Pine Valley experienced an unprecedented early summer heat wave. The garden's carefully planted herbs wilted under the scorching sun, and the newly renovated mill building's air conditioning struggled to keep up with the temperature.

"The bread won't proof properly in this heat," Helena fretted, checking the test kitchen's thermometers for the hundredth time. "And the chocolate work for the advanced classes..."

"Will be fine," Margaret assured her, adjusting the vintage fans they'd installed to maintain air circulation. "Remember what Mother always said about challenging conditions?"

"They build character," Helena and Stephanie recited together, sharing a knowing smile.

The past months had transformed both the town and their lives. The old mill now housed state-of-the-art teaching kitchens alongside preserved historical elements, creating a space that bridged past and present. Jack's veterinary clinic had expanded to include a lecture hall and student housing in the renovated carriage house behind the main building.

But it was the garden that had become the heart of everything. Despite the heat, the carefully planned beds flourished, Elizabeth's original design proving remarkably adaptable to modern needs. Heritage herbs grew alongside innovative hybrids, much like Sweet Pine Valley itself – honoring tradition while embracing change.

"Look who I found wandering around town square," Jack's voice carried from the garden path. He approached with a distinguished-looking gentleman who made Helena straighten suddenly.

"Michel?" she gasped. "Michel DuBois?"

The legendary French chef, Helena's former mentor and head of Le Cordon Bleu's international programs, smiled warmly. "I had to see this remarkable place for myself. When your proposal crossed my desk, Helena, I could hardly believe it was from the same woman who once claimed small towns were culinary wastelands."

Before Helena could respond, Tessa came bounding down the path, her excitement over visitors overcoming her usual reserve. To everyone's surprise, Michel knelt to greet her, speaking soft French to the delighted dachshund.

"Ah, you see?" he smiled up at them. "Even the dogs in Sweet Pine Valley have excellent taste. Now, show me everything. I want to understand how this little town has captured not only Helena Drake's heart but apparently the imagination of the entire culinary world."

The tour that followed revealed how much they'd accomplished. The mill's teaching kitchens gleamed with both modern equipment and carefully preserved historical elements. The garden's organized chaos told stories of growth and adaptation. Jack's clinic hummed with preparation for incoming students.

"And here," Stephanie led them into the bakery's newly expanded teaching space, "is where it all started. Where Elizabeth Fields first began teaching, and where Sophie Drake learned to bake."

Michel moved through the space slowly, touching equipment both old and new with reverent hands. "This is not just a school you're creating," he said finally. "This is not just a program. This is... how do you say... a renaissance. A rebirth of something precious."

"That's what we hoped for," Jack said, wrapping an arm around Stephanie. "Not just preserving the past, but giving it new life."

"Which is why I'm here," Michel turned to face them. "Le Cordon Bleu wants to expand our involvement beyond the current plans. We want to establish Sweet Pine Valley as our primary American heritage cooking campus. All our international students interested in American culinary traditions would come here."

The silence that followed was broken only by Tessa's gentle whine, sensing the tension in the room.

"That would mean..." Helena started.

"More students, yes. More facilities eventually. But," Michel held up a hand seeing their concerned faces, "all developed in keeping with what you've created here. We don't want to change Sweet Pine Valley – we want to learn from it."

Before anyone could respond, Sarah burst in, her face flushed with excitement. "The wedding designer is here! She's brought the sample materials and... oh!" She stopped short seeing Michel. "I'm so sorry, I didn't mean to interrupt..."

"Non, non," Michel smiled. "This is perfect timing. A wedding, you say? When?"

"December," Stephanie said softly. "In the garden, where Elizabeth used to teach."

"Ah! Then you must let me help. Consider it Le Cordon Bleu's gift – we will create a wedding feast that honors both tradition and innovation, just like Sweet Pine Valley itself."

The next few hours were a whirlwind of planning and possibility. The wedding designer, a renowned expert in vintage celebrations, fell in love with their vision of blending old and new. Michel and Helena debated menu possibilities that would showcase both French technique and American heritage recipes.

But it was Margaret who brought the most surprising contribution. From her seemingly bottomless collection of family treasures, she produced Sophie's wedding album.

"Look," she pointed to a faded photograph. "Mother and Elizabeth on the morning of the wedding, in this very kitchen. They're making the same bread recipe we used that day in spring when everything seemed overwhelming."

The photograph showed the two women, flour-dusted and laughing, clearly sharing a moment of joy despite whatever challenges they faced.

"That's what we need to remember," Stephanie said suddenly. "Through all these changes, all these opportunities – it's about moments like this. People coming together, sharing what they love, building something that lasts."

"Speaking of building something that lasts," Tom appeared in the doorway, "the historical society's architect just finished the final inspection of both houses. We're officially designated as historic landmarks, but with provisions for continued evolution of the properties' uses. They specifically cited the educational programs as being in keeping with Elizabeth and Sophie's legacy."

The day continued to unfold with a mix of planning and reminiscence. Michel explored every corner of their expanding campus, offering suggestions that somehow managed to enhance rather than change their vision. The wedding designer sketched possibilities that captured both their love story and Sweet Pine Valley's heritage.

As evening approached, bringing some relief from the heat, they gathered in the garden. Helena's culinary students would arrive in three days, Jack's veterinary students in a week. The mill's kitchens were ready, the clinic's new facilities prepared, the garden bursting with life despite the challenging weather.

"I have something for you," Margaret said softly to Stephanie. She held out a small, worn book. "Mother's personal recipe journal. Not the professional one – her private one, where she wrote about her dreams for the future. Her hopes for what Sweet Pine Valley could become."

Stephanie opened it carefully, Jack reading over her shoulder. Sophie's elegant handwriting filled the pages with more than just recipes – there were notes about teaching methods, observations about community needs, dreams for future generations.

"She wrote this on the day she finished her training with Elizabeth," Margaret pointed to one particular entry. "'Today I understand that success isn't measured in grand achievements, but in the small moments where we help others find their path. Elizabeth hasn't just taught me to bake – she's shown me how to build a legacy of love and learning.'"

Michel, who had been quietly observing, spoke up. "This is what we want our students to understand. Not just technique, not just tradition, but the heart of what makes a place like Sweet Pine Valley special."

"It's what we want the veterinary students to learn too," Jack added. "That being part of a community means more than just practicing medicine."

As the sun set, casting long shadows through the garden, they shared a meal at the old table Elizabeth had used for her outdoor classes. Helena and Michel collaborated on a spontaneous feast that combined French sophistication with small-town charm. Sarah and Tom shared their latest wedding plans, while Margaret told more stories of Sophie's early days in Sweet Pine Valley.

Stephanie looked around at their gathered family – both blood and chosen – and felt the rightness of everything they'd built. Yes, changes were coming. Yes, their little town would grow and evolve. But the heart of what made Sweet Pine Valley special would remain.

"Penny for your thoughts?" Jack whispered, squeezing her hand under the table.

"Just thinking about legacy," she replied. "About how Elizabeth and Sophie probably sat at this very table, planning their own dreams for the future."

"And now we're planning ours," he smiled. "Though I doubt they imagined their little teaching garden would become an international culinary campus."

"Or that their stories would inspire so many others," Helena added, overhearing them. "Michel has already suggested a book series about American regional cooking, starting with Sweet Pine Valley's heritage recipes."

"The first volume," Michel raised his glass, "will be dedicated to Elizabeth Fields and Sophie Drake – two women who understood that the greatest legacy is the one that keeps growing."

As night fell, fireflies began to dance in the garden. Someone started playing music from the cottage – old folk tunes mixed with modern melodies, just like everything else in their evolving world.

"To Sweet Pine Valley," Margaret proposed a toast. "Where past and future meet in perfect harmony."

"To dreams that grow," Helena added, her usual reserve softened by the evening's magic.

"To love that lasts," Sarah and Tom chimed in.

"To the next chapter," Jack whispered to Stephanie.

Tomorrow would bring more preparations, more changes, more steps toward their expanding future. But tonight, in the garden where so many dreams had taken root, they celebrated the simple joy of being exactly where they were meant to be.

After all, as Sophie had written in her journal: "The sweetest moments are those where past and future touch, where dreams meet reality, and where love finds its truest home."

Chapter 15

Hearts Come Home

December returned to Sweet Pine Valley like a carefully wrapped gift, bringing with it soft snow and the promise of dreams fulfilled. The morning of Stephanie and Jack's wedding dawned clear and cold, the kind of crystalline winter day that seemed created especially for new beginnings.

Stephanie stood at her bedroom window in the Victorian house, watching early light paint the garden in shades of rose and gold. Despite the winter, it remained a place of magic – Helena and Margaret had worked miracles with evergreen garlands and twinkling lights, transforming the dormant beds into a winter wonderland.

"Everything's ready," Helena announced, entering with what appeared to be her grandmother's cookbook. She looked different today – softer somehow in a deep blue dress that matched the winter sky. "The students have finished setting up the reception in the mill, Michel's team has the menu under control, and Sarah's handling the last-minute decorations."

"And Tessa?" Stephanie asked, knowing their little dachshund had a special role to play.

"Being pampered by the groomer," Sarah answered, arriving with Stephanie's wedding dress – a perfect blend of vintage charm and modern elegance, created using lace from both Elizabeth's and Sophie's wedding gowns. "Though she's more interested in the treat bag we're attaching to her ring bearer pillow."

The house hummed with preparation. Downstairs, they could hear Jack's parents greeting early arrivals, while Tom directed the photography team to the best spots for capturing both the ceremony and the historic properties. The bakery's window displayed a recreation of Elizabeth's original wedding cake design, updated with Helena's modern techniques.

"Look what Margaret found this morning," Helena held out Sophie's cookbook, opened to a particular page. There, pressed between recipes for wedding cookies, was a dried sprig of rosemary. A note in Sophie's handwriting read: "From Elizabeth's wedding bouquet – she said rosemary was for remembrance and new beginnings."

"We found fresh rosemary in the greenhouse this morning," Margaret added, joining them. "Still blooming despite the winter. Elizabeth would say that's a sign."

As if summoned by the mention of signs, Mrs. Henderson appeared with a small wooden box. "The historical society wanted you to have this today," she said, opening it to reveal a collection of small items: a silver spoon with Elizabeth's initials, a delicate lace handkerchief that had belonged to Sophie, and a packet of letters they hadn't discovered before.

"They're from Elizabeth to Sophie," Mrs. Henderson explained, "written the winter Sophie was considering leaving Vermont for a position in New York. Elizabeth wrote about how some places claim our hearts, how some loves are meant to root us where we can grow best."

Stephanie felt tears threatening as she read the letters. Elizabeth's words, written so long ago, seemed meant for this very day: "My dearest Sophie, remember that the grandest dreams often bloom in the smallest gardens, and the truest love stories are those written in familiar soil."

The morning passed in a blur of preparation and precious moments. Helena and Margaret worked together to create Sophie's traditional wedding morning bread, filling both houses with the scent of home and history. Sarah wove tiny lights through the garden's winter branches, making them shimmer like stars caught in crystal.

Finally, it was time. Stephanie stood at the garden's entrance, her father beside her, watching as their gathered loved ones found their places along the illuminated paths. Jack waited beneath an arch woven with evergreens and white roses, looking handsome and slightly nervous in his wedding suit.

Tessa preceded them down the aisle, proudly carrying a small pillow with their rings. She'd overcome her timidity entirely, prancing between the guests with dignity despite her festive collar. The rings themselves were special – Jack's a simple band that had belonged to Elizabeth's husband, Stephanie's the delicate snowflake ring that had found its way home.

The ceremony blended traditional elements with their own unique touches. They exchanged vows beneath the arch where Elizabeth had once taught her students about growth and possibility. Their words honored both their personal journey and the legacy they'd become part of:

"In this garden where dreams have taken root for generations," Jack promised, "I choose you as my partner in all seasons."

"In this place where past meets future," Stephanie responded, her voice steady despite her tears, "I promise to grow with you, dream with you, build with you."

After the ceremony, the celebration moved to the mill building, now a stunning blend of historic architecture and modern elegance. Michel's team had outdone themselves, creating a feast that told Sweet Pine Valley's story through food. Each dish combined traditional recipes with contemporary presentations, much like the town itself.

The wedding cake stood as a masterpiece of collaboration – Helena and Stephanie had recreated Elizabeth's original design but added their own touches. Each tier told part of their story: the base featured piped designs from Sophie's notebook, the middle displayed sugar sculptures of local landmarks, and the top held a miniature recreation of the bakery's famous Christmas window display.

"If Elizabeth could see this," Margaret mused, watching the celebration unfold, "she'd say her dreams for Sweet Pine Valley had bloomed beyond imagining."

"I think she can see it," Mrs. Henderson smiled, nodding toward the mill's windows where snow had begun to fall gently. "Some might call it coincidence that it started snowing at exactly the moment you said 'I do' – just like it did at Elizabeth's wedding, according to town records."

The evening flowed like a perfectly crafted recipe, each moment adding to the whole. Helena's culinary students served alongside Michel's team, while Jack's veterinary students, who had become part of the community, helped manage the celebrations. The townspeople mingled with internationally renowned chefs and agricultural experts, all brought together by the magic of Sweet Pine Valley.

As night deepened, Stephanie and Jack shared their first dance in the garden, now lit by thousands of tiny lights. The snow continued to fall gently, adding its own sparkle to the scene.

"Happy?" Jack whispered as they swayed together.

"More than I ever dreamed possible," Stephanie replied, watching their gathered family and friends through the mill's warm windows. Helena was teaching Margaret's great-grandchildren how to properly hold a piping bag, while Michel discussed local farming techniques with Dr. Thompson. Sarah and Tom danced nearby, as much in love as ever.

"Look," Jack nodded toward a quiet corner where Tessa had gathered all the children, supervising their enjoyment of specially made dog-safe wedding cookies. "Who would have thought our timid little rescue would become such a confident hostess?"

"She learned from the best," Stephanie smiled, thinking of her own journey from uncertain newcomer to confident community member. "We all did."

Later that night, after the guests had gone and the cleanup was left for tomorrow, they gathered in the bakery's kitchen. Helena made hot chocolate using Sophie's recipe, while Margaret shared one last wedding tradition.

"Mother and Elizabeth started this," she explained, pulling out two small journals. "On every wedding they catered, they would write their hopes for the couple's future. I found these in the cottage attic – blank ones, waiting to be filled."

One by one, they wrote their wishes. Helena wrote about the power of finding where you belong. Sarah and Tom wished for a life filled with sweet surprises. Margaret wrote about the strength of roots and the beauty of growth.

"Your turn," Jack handed one journal to Stephanie. "What do you wish for our future?"

Stephanie thought for a moment, then wrote: "May our love story continue to blend the best of past and present, like the perfect recipe handed down through generations but made new with each creation. May we always remember that the grandest dreams can bloom in small-town gardens, and the truest homes are built one heart at a time."

The snow continued to fall outside, adding another layer of white to their winter wonderland. Through the bakery window, they could see the garden waiting for spring, knowing it would bloom again with new stories, new students, new dreams.

"To Elizabeth and Sophie," Helena raised her hot chocolate. "Who knew that sometimes the sweetest path leads you right back home."

"To Sweet Pine Valley," Margaret added. "Where old dreams find new life."

"To us," Jack whispered to Stephanie. "And all the chapters yet to come."

As midnight approached, they made their way back through the gently falling snow to their Victorian house. The porch lights welcomed them home, and through the windows, they could see their Christmas tree glowing softly.

"You know what Elizabeth wrote in her last diary entry?" Stephanie said as they paused on the porch. "She said, 'The greatest gift we can leave future generations is not just our recipes or our gardens, but our faith in love's ability to bloom wherever it's planted.'"

Jack pulled her close, snowflakes catching in her hair like tiny stars. "She was right. Look at everything that's bloomed here – the school, the clinic, the garden..."

"Our love story," Stephanie finished, reaching up to kiss him as the church bells began to chime midnight.

Inside, Tessa waited by the fire, ready to begin this new chapter with them. The house settled around them with the contentment of a place that had seen many loves, many dreams, many new beginnings.

Tomorrow would bring more students, more recipes, more stories to add to Sweet Pine Valley's rich tapestry. But tonight, in the quiet of their first moments as husband and wife, they were simply home.

After all, as Elizabeth had written and Sophie had proven, the sweetest stories are those that find their way back to where they belong, blooming ever new in familiar soil, growing ever stronger in love's gentle grace.

Epilogue

Sweet Tomorrows

Two Years Later

The garden bloomed with late summer flowers as dawn painted the Victorian house in golden light. Stephanie rocked gently in the porch swing, cradling six-month-old Elizabeth Sophie Carter, named for the two remarkable women who had unknowingly shaped their lives. The baby dozed peacefully, one tiny hand clutching her mother's apron – the same vintage-style apron Helena had given Stephanie when she announced her pregnancy.

"There's my girls," Jack whispered, emerging from the house with two cups of coffee and an enthusiastic escort of dachshunds. Tessa, now the dignified senior dog, supervised her younger companion, a recent rescue named Cookie who had stolen their hearts at the clinic three months ago.

"Did we wake you?" Stephanie accepted her coffee gratefully.

"The dynamic duo here decided dawn was the perfect time for their morning patrol," Jack smiled, watching as Tessa showed Cookie the proper way to inspect the garden's perimeter. "Though I think they were just excited about today's special breakfast."

Today marked the second anniversary of the Sweet Pine Valley Culinary and Veterinary Education Center's opening. To celebrate, they were hosting a community breakfast in the garden, combining the traditions of both programs. Helena's advanced baking students would serve alongside Jack's veterinary interns, while local families shared their own heritage recipes.

"Hard to believe how much has changed in two years," Stephanie mused, adjusting little Elizabeth as she stirred. "The programs, the cookbook series, the garden tours..."

"The newest member of the Carter family," Jack added, gently touching their daughter's cheek. "Though I didn't expect her to inherit Helena's early-rising habits."

As if summoned by her name, Helena appeared through the garden gate, already immaculate in her chef's whites despite the early hour. She carried a basket of fresh croissants and what appeared to be a new dog toy.

"For my favorite taste-tester," she announced, presenting the toy to Cookie, who accepted it with delicate manners that proved Tessa's mentoring. "And for my favorite namesake..." She produced a tiny chef's hat, perfectly sized for baby Elizabeth.

"From Paris," she explained. "Michel had it specially made when I told him she's already showing interest in the kitchen." This was true – Elizabeth seemed fascinated by the baking process, watching intently from her carrier whenever Stephanie worked.

The morning unfolded like a well-loved recipe. Sarah and Tom arrived with their own news – they were expecting twins in winter. Margaret, now a permanent resident in the cottage's guest suite, brought out Sophie's special occasion china for the breakfast.

Students and townspeople began arriving, filling the garden with laughter and conversation. Cookie proved to be an excellent hostess, while Tessa maintained her role as quality control supervisor, especially near the pastry tables.

"Look who made it," Jack nudged Stephanie, nodding toward the gate where Michel DuBois entered with an elegant older woman.

"Julia?" Helena's voice carried surprise and joy. "Julia Child's great-niece? But you said you couldn't leave Paris..."

"And miss seeing what you've all created here?" Julia smiled. "Besides, I have a proposition. The Julia Child Foundation is interested in establishing a permanent partnership with your programs. We want to help preserve and promote American culinary heritage, and Sweet Pine Valley seems the perfect place to center those efforts."

As they discussed details, baby Elizabeth woke fully, her eyes bright with interest at all the activity. Cookie immediately reported for baby-monitoring duty, positioning herself protectively near the infant's chair, while Tessa supervised them both.

"She's going to be a chef," Helena declared, watching Elizabeth reach for a nearby croissant.

"Or a veterinarian," Jack countered as their daughter showed equal interest in Cookie's gentle affection.

"Or both," Stephanie suggested. "After all, Sweet Pine Valley is all about combining different paths."

The morning sun rose higher, warming the garden where so many dreams had taken root. The Victorian house stood proud behind them, its windows reflecting golden light. From the mill came the sounds of preparation for the day's classes, while the clinic's new bell chimed softly in the morning breeze.

"You know what Elizabeth Fields wrote about legacies?" Margaret said, joining them with fresh coffee. "That they're not just about passing down what we've learned, but about leaving space for future generations to add their own chapters."

Looking around at their gathered family – both blood and chosen – Stephanie felt the truth of those words. Helena discussing future programs with Julia, Sarah and Tom planning their own family's growth, the students learning and adding their own innovations to traditional methods, and their daughter, named for the women who had started it all, beginning her own story.

"To Sweet Pine Valley," Jack raised his coffee cup. "Where every ending is just a new beginning."

"To family," Helena added, her usual reserve melting as baby Elizabeth grabbed her finger.

"To love," Sarah and Tom chimed in, sharing their own special glow.

"To tomorrow," Stephanie whispered, leaning into Jack's embrace as their daughter laughed at Cookie's gentle antics while Tessa maintained her dignified oversight.

The garden bloomed around them, eternal yet ever-changing, like love itself. And somewhere, perhaps, Elizabeth Fields and Sophie Drake smiled down on the legacy they'd planted – a legacy that continued to grow, one heart, one dream, and one sweet moment at a time.

Patti Petrone Miller

PRISE FOR THE AUTHOR

Praise For Author "Patti Petrone Miller's books hit different from your typical feel-good stories. Sure, Hallmark's got their formula down pat, but Miller brings something fresh to the table - authentic characters that actually feel like people you know, dealing with real-life stuff while still keeping things wonderfully uplifting.
I honestly get the same warm fuzzies reading her books as I do curling up with hot cocoa for a Hallmark marathon, but without all the predictable plot points we've seen a million times. She's nailed that sweet spot between heartwarming and genuine that's super hard to find these days. If you're looking for stories that'll leave you smiling but don't make you roll your eyes at how perfect everything is, Miller's your girl. She's got that special touch that makes you feel like you're hanging out with friends rather than just reading about characters. Move over, Hallmark - there's a new queen of wholesome in town!"

ABOUT THE AUTHOR

Ladies and gentlemen, step right up to "Where the Magic Happens" - a literary circus that'll make your bookshelf do backflips!

Meet Patti, the ringmaster of this wordy wonderland! She's not just an Executive Producer; she's a word-wrangling wizard, conjuring up an animated TV series based on "ELLIOT FINDS A HOME." It's the tail-wagging tale of a thumbs-up pup and his silent sidekick, proving that you don't need words when you've got opposable digits and a heart of gold!

Hold onto your bestseller lists, folks! This Polygon Entertainment superstar has hit the USA TODAY jackpot and Amazon's #1 spot more times than a cat has lives. With 7 dozen books under her belt, she's got more genres than a chameleon has colors. From Urban Fantasy to Horror, she's been spinning yarns longer than your grandma's knitting needles!

But wait, there's more! Patti's life is like a celebrity bingo card:

She rocked "Romper Room" at 4, probably making the other kids look like amateur rompers.

She rubbed elbows with Captain Kangaroo and Mr. Green Jeans. (No word on whether the jeans were actually green.)

She shared a train ride and a sandwich with Sidney Poitier. Talk about a meal ticket to stardom!

Patti Petrone Miller

She high-fived President Nixon at the circus. Who knew the circus could get any more political?

She went to school with David Copperfield. We assume she didn't disappear during attendance.

She roller-skated with pre-famous John Travolta. Grease lightning, indeed!

She sipped cocoa with Abe Vigoda. Fish never tasted so sweet!

When she's not busy being a literary legend, Patti's juggling roles faster than a circus performer. Teacher, grandma, furparent - she does it all with a smile that could light up a haunted house.

knitting needles!

But wait, there's more! Patti's life is like a celebrity bingo card:

She rocked "Romper Room" at 4, probably making the other kids look like amateur rompers.

She rubbed elbows with Captain Kangaroo and Mr. Green Jeans. (No word on whether the jeans were actually green.)

She shared a train ride and a sandwich with Sidney Poitier. Talk about a meal ticket to stardom!

She high-fived President Nixon at the circus. Who knew the circus could get any more political?

She went to school with David Copperfield. We assume she didn't disappear during attendance.

She roller-skated with pre-famous John Travolta. Grease lightning, indeed!

Barking Up The Wrong Bakery, Thanksgiving

She sipped cocoa with Abe Vigoda. Fish never tasted so sweet!

When she's not busy being a literary legend, Patti's juggling roles faster than a circus performer. Teacher, grandma, furparent - she does it all with a smile that could light up a haunted house.

Speaking of haunted houses, meet the "Queen of Halloween" herself! This Wiccan High Priestess is stirring up stories spookier than a skeleton's dance moves. Her books are flying off the shelves faster than witches on broomsticks, so follow her on social media or risk missing out on the hocus-pocus!

So, come one, come all, to Patti's phantasmagorical world of words! It's more exciting than a roller coaster, more magical than a rabbit in a hat, and more diverse than a box of assorted chocolates. Don't be shy - step into the spotlight and join the literary party where the pages turn themselves and the stories never end!

www.ingramcontent.com/pod-product-compliance
Lightning Source LLC
LaVergne TN
LVHW041611070526
838199LV00052B/3086